Grass for His Pillow

LORD FUJIWARA'S TREASURES

FIREBIRD

WHERE FANTASY TAKES FLIGHT™

Across the Nightingale Floor *Episode One: The Sword of the Warrior*	Lian Hearn
Across the Nightingale Floor *Episode Two: Journey to Inuyama*	Lian Hearn
The Blue Sword	Robin McKinley
Firebirds: An Anthology of Original Fantasy and Science Fiction	Sharyn November, ed.
Grass for His Pillow *Episode Two: The Way Through the Snow*	Lian Hearn
The Green Man: Tales from the Mythic Forest	Ellen Datlow and Terri Windling, eds.
The Mount	Carol Emshwiller
The Neverending Story	Michael Ende
The Riddle of the Wren	Charles de Lint
The Safe-Keeper's Secret	Sharon Shinn
Spindle's End	Robin McKinley
Tamsin	Peter S. Beagle
Waifs and Strays	Charles de Lint
Waters Luminous and Deep: Shorter Fictions	Meredith Ann Pierce

BOOKS BY LIAN HEARN

TALES OF THE OTORI

Across the Nightingale Floor
Episode One: The Sword of the Warrior
Episode Two: Journey to Inuyama

Grass for His Pillow
Episode One: Lord Fujiwara's Treasures
Episode Two: The Way Through the Snow

Brilliance of the Moon
Episode One: Battle for Maruyama
Episode Two: Scars of Victory

OTORI
CLAN

MARUYAMA
CLAN

SEISHUU
CLAN

SHIRAKAWA
CLAN

TOHAN
CLAN

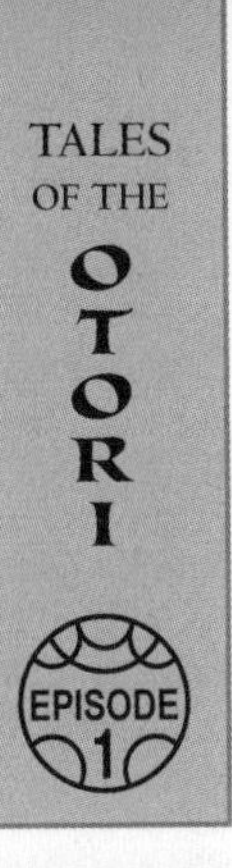

Grass for His Pillow

LORD FUJIWARA'S TREASURES

LIAN HEARN

FIREBIRD
AN IMPRINT OF PENGUIN GROUP (USA) INC.

FIREBIRD
Published by the Penguin Group
Penguin Group (USA) Inc., 345 Hudson Street, New York, New York 10014, U.S.A.
Penguin Group (Canada), 10 Alcorn Avenue, Toronto, Ontario, Canada M4V 3B2
(a division of Pearson Penguin Canada Inc.)

Registered Offices: Penguin Books Ltd, 80 Strand, London WC2R 0RL, England

This is a work of fiction. Names, characters, places, and incidents either are the product of the author's imagination or are used fictitiously, and any resemblance to actual persons, living or dead, business establishments, events, or locales is entirely coincidental.

The author gratefully acknowledges permission to quote from *From the Country of Eight Islands* by Hiroaki Sato, translated by Burton Watson. Used by permission of Doubleday, a division of Random House, Inc.

Excerpt from "Kinuta" from *Japanese Noh Drama*, edited by Royall Tyler, Penguin Classics.

First published in the United States of America by Riverhead Books,
a member of Penguin Group (USA) Inc., 2003
Published by Firebird, an imprint of Penguin Group (USA) Inc., 2005

1 3 5 7 9 10 8 6 4 2

Clan symbols by Jackie Aher
Calligraphy drawn by Ms. Sugiyama Kazuko
Map by Xiangyi Mo

THE LIBRARY OF CONGRESS HAS CATALOGUED THE RIVERHEAD EDITION AS FOLLOWS:
Hearn, Lian.
Grass for his pillow / Lian Hearn.
p. cm.—(Tales of the Otori ; bk. 2)
Sequel to: Across the nightingale floor.
ISBN 1-57322-251-8
1. Teenage boys—Fiction. 2. Orphans—Fiction. 3. Japan—Fiction. I. Title.
PR9619.3.H3725G73 2003 2003043215
823'.914—dc21

ISBN 0-14-240423-3

Printed in China

FOREWORD

These events took place in the year following the death of Otori Shigeru in the Tohan stronghold of Inuyama. The leader of the Tohan clan, Iida Sadamu, was killed in revenge by Shigeru's adopted son, Otori Takeo, or so it was widely believed, and the Tohan overthrown by Arai Daiichi, one of the Seishuu clan from Kumamoto, who took advantage of the chaos following the fall of Inuyama to seize control of the Three Countries. Arai had hoped to form an alliance with Takeo and arrange his marriage to Shirakawa Kaede, now the heir to the Maruyama and Shirakawa domains.

However, torn between Shigeru's last commands and the demands of his real father's family, the Kikuta of the Tribe, Takeo gave up his inheritance and marriage with Kaede, with whom he was deeply in love, to go with the Tribe, feeling himself bound to them by blood and by oath.

Otori Shigeru was buried at Terayama, a remote mountain temple in the heart of the Middle Country. After the battles of Inuyama and Kushimoto, Arai visited the temple to pay his respects to his fallen ally and to confirm the new alliances. Here Takeo and Kaede met for the last time.

The Three Countries

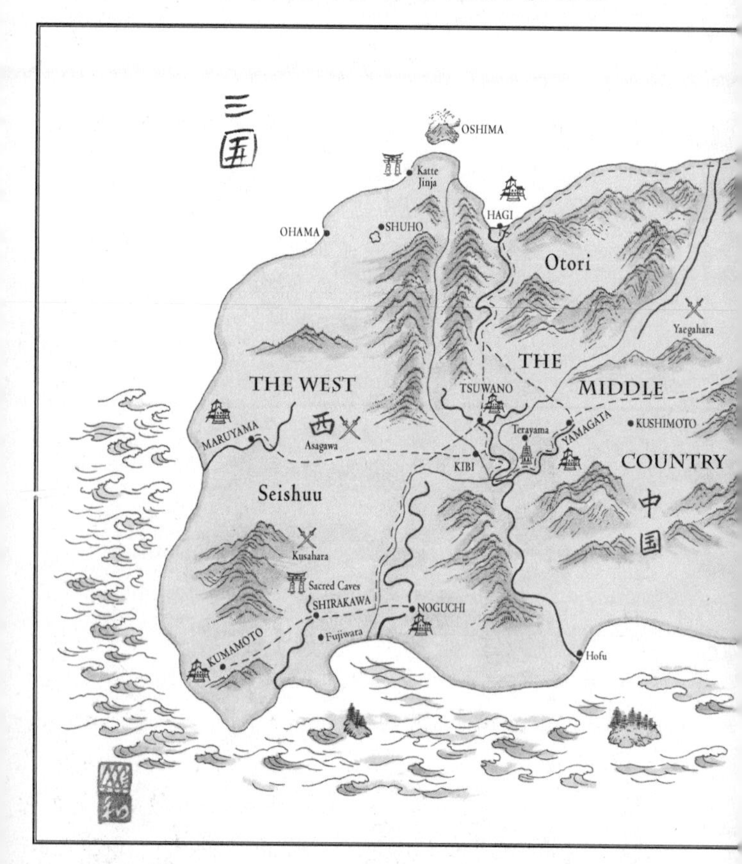

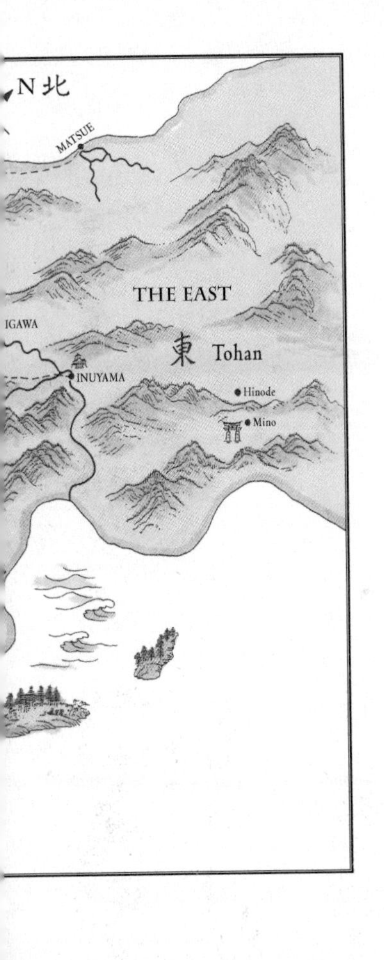

fief boundaries

fief boundaries before Yaegahara

high road

battlefields

castletown

shrine

temple

CHARACTERS

The Clans

THE OTORI

(Middle Country; castle town: Hagi)

Otori Shigeru: rightful heir to the clan
Otori Takeshi: his younger brother, murdered by the Tohan clan **(d.)**
Otori Takeo: (born Tomasu) his adopted son
Otori Shigemori: Shigeru's father, killed at the battle of Yaegahara **(d.)**
Otori Ichiro: a distant relative, Shigeru and Takeo's teacher

Chiyo
Haruka: maids in the household

Shiro: a carpenter

Otori Shoichi: Shigeru's uncle, now lord of the clan
Otori Masahiro: Shoichi's younger brother
Otori Yoshitomi: Masahiro's son

Miyoshi Kahei: brothers, friends of Takeo
Miyoshi Gemba

Miyoshi Satoru: their father, captain of the guard in Hagi castle

Endo Chikara: a senior retainer

Terada Fumifusa: a pirate
Terada Fumio: his son, friend of Takeo

Ryoma: a fisherman, Masahiro's illegitimate son

THE TOHAN

(The East; castle town: Inuyama)

Iida Sadamu: lord of the clan
Iida Nariaki: Sadamu's cousin

Ando, Abe: Iida's retainers

Lord Noguchi: an ally
Lady Noguchi: his wife
Junko: a servant in Noguchi castle

THE SEISHUU

(An alliance of several ancient families in the West; main castle towns: Kumamoto and Maruyama)

Arai Daiichi: a warlord

Niwa Satoru: a retainer
Akita Tsutomu: a retainer
Sonoda Mitsuru: Akita's nephew
Maruyama Naomi: head of the Maruyama domain, Shigeru's lover

Mariko: her daughter
Sachie: her maid

Sugita Haruki: a retainer
Sugita Hiroshi: his nephew
Sakai Masaki: Hiroshi's cousin

Lord Shirakawa
Kaede: Shirakawa's eldest daughter, Lady Maruyama's cousin
Ai, Hana: Shirakawa's daughters

Ayame
Manami
Akane: maids in the household

Amano Tenzo: a Shirakawa retainer

Shoji Kiyoshi: senior retainer to Lord Shirakawa

The Tribe

THE MUTO FAMILY

Muto Kenji: Takeo's teacher, the master
Muto Shizuka: Kenji's niece, Arai's mistress, and Kaede's companion
Zenko, Taku: her sons
Muto Seiko: Kenji's wife
Muto Yuki: their daughter
Muto Yuzuru: a cousin

Kana
Miyabi: maids

THE KIKUTA FAMILY

Kikuta Isamu: Takeo's real father (d.)
Kikuta Kotaro: his cousin, the Master
Kikuta Gosaburo: Kotaro's younger brother
Kikuta Akio: their nephew
Kikuta Hajime: a wrestler
Sadako: a maid

THE KURODA FAMILY

Kuroda Shintaro: a famous assassin
Kondo Kiichi
Imai Kazuo
Kudo Keiko

Others

Lord Fujiwara: a nobleman, exiled from the capital
Mamoru: his protégé and companion
Ono Rieko: his cousin
Murita: a retainer

Matsuda Shingen: the abbot at Terayama
Kubo Makoto: a monk, Takeo's closest friend

Jin-emon: a bandit

Jiro: a farmer's son

Jo-An: an outcast

Horses

Raku: gray with black mane and tail, Takeo's first horse, given by him to Kaede
Kyu: black, Shigeru's horse, disappeared in Inuyama
Aoi: black, half brother to Kyu
Ki: Amano's chestnut
Shun: Takeo's bay, a very clever horse

bold = main characters
(d.) = character died before the start of *Across the Nightingale Floor, Episode 1*

貧窮問答の歌一首

風雑へ　雨降る夜の　雨雑へ
雪降る夜は　術もなく　寒くし
あれば　堅塩を　取りつづしろひ
糟湯酒　うち啜ろひて　咳かひ
鼻びしびしに　しかとあらぬ　髭
かき撫でて　我を除きて　人はあらじと
誇ろへど　寒くしあれば　麻衾
引き被り　布肩衣　有りのことごと
服襲へども　寒き夜すらを　我
よりも　貧しき人の　父母は　飢ゑ
寒ゆらむ　……後略……

「万葉集」巻五
八九二

On nights when, wind mixing in, the rain falls,
On nights when, rain mixing in, the snow falls

YAMANOUE NO OKURA:
A DIALOGUE ON POVERTY.
FROM *THE COUNTRY OF THE EIGHT ISLANDS*
TRANS: HIROAKI SATO

Grass for His Pillow

LORD FUJIWARA'S TREASURES

·1·

Shirakawa Kaede lay deeply asleep in the state close to unconsciousness that the Kikuta can deliver with their gaze. The night passed, the stars paled as dawn came, the sounds of the temple rose and fell around her, but she did not stir. She did not hear her companion, Shizuka, call anxiously to her from time to time, trying to wake her. She did not feel Shizuka's hand on her forehead. She did not hear Lord Arai Daiichi's men as they came with increasing impatience to the veranda, telling Shizuka that the warlord was waiting to speak to Lady Shirakawa. Her breathing was peaceful and calm, her features as still as a mask's.

Toward evening the quality of her sleep seemed to change.

Her eyelids flickered and her lips appeared to smile. Her fingers, which had been curled gently against her palms, spread.

Be patient. He will come for you.

Kaede was dreaming that she had been turned to ice. The words echoed lucidly in her head. There was no fear in the dream, just the feeling of being held by something cool and white in a world that was silent, frozen, and enchanted.

Her eyes opened.

It was still light. The shadows told her it was evening. A wind bell rang softly, once, and then the air was still. The day she had no recollection of must have been a warm one. Her skin was damp beneath her hair. Birds were chattering from the eaves, and she could hear the clip of the swallows' beaks as they caught the last insects of the day. Soon they would fly south. It was already autumn.

The sound of the birds reminded her of the painting Takeo had given her, many weeks before, at this same place, a sketch of a wild forest bird that had made her think of freedom; it had been lost along with everything else she possessed, her wedding robes, all her other clothes, when the castle at Inuyama burned. She possessed nothing. Shizuka had found some old robes for her at the house they had stayed in, and had borrowed combs and other things. She had never been in such a place before, a merchant's house, smelling of fermenting soy, full of people, whom she tried to keep away from, though every now and then the maids came to peep at her through the screens.

She was afraid everyone would see what had happened to her on the night the castle fell. She had killed a man, she had lain with another, she had fought alongside him, wielding the dead man's sword. She could not believe she had done these things. Sometimes she thought she was bewitched, as people said. They said of her that any man who desired her died—and it was true. Men had died. But not Takeo.

Ever since she had been assaulted by the guard when she was a hostage in Noguchi Castle, she had been afraid of all men. Her terror of Iida had driven her to defend herself against him, but she had had no fear of Takeo. She had only wanted to hold him closer. Since their first meeting in Tsuwano, her body had longed for his. She had wanted him to touch her, she had wanted the feel of his skin against hers. Now, as she remembered that night, she understood with renewed clarity that she could marry no one but him, she would love no one but him. *I will be patient,* she promised. But where had those words come from?

She turned her head slightly and saw Shizuka's outline on the edge of the veranda. Beyond the woman rose the ancient trees of the shrine. The air smelled of cedars and dust. The temple bell tolled the evening hour. Kaede did not speak. She did not want to talk to anyone, or hear any voice. She wanted to go back to that place of ice where she had been sleeping.

Then, beyond the specks of dust that floated in the last rays of the sun, she saw something: a spirit, she thought, yet not only a spirit, for it had substance; it was there, undeniable and real, gleaming like fresh snow. She stared, half rose, but in the moment that she recognized her, the White Goddess, the all-compassionate, the all-merciful, was gone.

"What is it?" Shizuka heard the movement and ran to her side. Kaede looked at Shizuka and saw the deep concern in her eyes. She realized how precious this woman had become to her—her closest, indeed her only friend.

"Nothing. A half dream."

"Are you all right? How do you feel?"

"I don't know. I feel . . ." Kaede's voice died away. She gazed at Shizuka for several moments. "Have I been asleep all day? What happened to me?"

"He shouldn't have done it to you," Shizuka said, her voice sharp with concern and anger.

"It was Takeo?"

Shizuka nodded. "I had no idea he had that skill. It's a trait of the Kikuta family."

"The last thing I remember is his eyes. We gazed at each other and then I fell asleep."

After a pause Kaede went on: "He's gone, hasn't he?"

"My uncle, Muto Kenji, and the Kikuta master Kotaro came for him last night," Shizuka replied.

"And I will never see him again?" Kaede remembered her desperation the previous night, before the long, deep sleep. She had begged Takeo not to leave her. She had been terrified of her future without him, angry and wounded by his rejection of her. But all that turbulence had been stilled.

"You must forget him," Shizuka said, taking Kaede's hand in hers and stroking it gently. "From now on, his life and yours cannot touch."

Kaede smiled slightly. *I cannot forget him,* she was thinking.

Nor can he ever be taken from me. I have slept in ice. I have seen the White Goddess.

"Are you all right?" Shizuka said again, with urgency. "Not many people survive the Kikuta sleep. They are usually dispatched before they wake. I don't know what it has done to you."

"It hasn't harmed me. But it has altered me in some way. I feel as if I don't know anything—as if I have to learn everything anew."

Shizuka knelt before her, puzzled, her eyes searching Kaede's face. "What will you do now? Where will you go? Will you return to Inuyama with Arai?"

"I think I should go home to my parents. I must see my mother. I'm so afraid she died while we were delayed in Inuyama for all that time. I will leave in the morning. I suppose you should inform Lord Arai."

"I understand your anxiety," Shizuka replied, "but Arai may be reluctant to let you go."

"Then I shall have to persuade him," Kaede said calmly. "First I must eat something. Will you ask them to prepare some food? And bring me some tea, please."

"Lady." Shizuka bowed to her and stepped off the

veranda. As she walked away Kaede heard the plaintive notes of a flute played by some unseen person in the garden behind the temple. She thought she knew the player, one of the young monks from the time when they had first visited the temple to view the famous Sesshu paintings, but she could not recall his name. The music spoke to her of the inevitability of suffering and loss. The trees stirred as the wind rose, and owls began to hoot from the mountain.

Shizuka came back with the tea and poured a cup for Kaede. She drank as if she were tasting it for the first time, every drop having its own distinct, smoky flavor against her tongue. And when the old woman who looked after guests brought rice and vegetables cooked with bean curd, it was as if she had never tasted food before. She marveled silently at the new powers that had been awakened within her.

"Lord Arai wishes to speak with you before the end of the day," Shizuka said. "I told him you were not well, but he insisted. If you do not feel like facing him now, I will go and tell him again."

"I am not sure we can treat Lord Arai in that fashion," Kaede said. "If he commands me, I must go to him."

"He is very angry," Shizuka said in a low voice. "He is

offended and outraged by Takeo's disappearance. He sees in it the loss of two important alliances. He will almost certainly have to fight the Otori now, without Takeo on his side. He'd hoped for a quick marriage between you—"

"Don't speak of it," Kaede interrupted. She finished the last of the rice, placed the eating sticks down on the tray, and bowed in thanks for the food.

Shizuka sighed. "Arai has no real understanding of the Tribe—how they work, what demands they place on those who belong to them."

"Did he never know that you were from the Tribe?"

"He knew I had ways of finding things out, of passing on messages. He was happy enough to make use of my skills in forming the alliance with Lord Shigeru and Lady Maruyama. He had heard of the Tribe, but like most people he thought they were little more than a guild. That they should have been involved in Iida's death shocked him profoundly, even though he profited from it." She paused and then said quietly, "He has lost all trust in me: I think he wonders how he slept with me so many times without being assassinated himself. Well, we will certainly never sleep together again. That is all over."

"Are you afraid of him? Has he threatened you?"

"He is furious with me," Shizuka replied. "He feels I have betrayed him—worse: made a fool out of him. I do not think he will ever forgive me." A bitter note crept into her voice. "I have been his closest confidante, his lover, his friend, since I was hardly more than a child. I have borne him two sons. Yet, he would have me put to death in an instant were it not for your presence."

"I will kill any man who tries to harm you," Kaede said.

Shizuka smiled. "How fierce you look when you say that!"

"Men die easily." Kaede's voice was flat. "From the prick of a needle, the thrust of a knife. You taught me that."

"But you are yet to use those skills, I hope," Shizuka replied, "though you fought well at Inuyama. Takeo owes his life to you."

Kaede was silent for a moment. Then she said in a low voice, "I did more than fight with the sword. You do not know all of it."

Shizuka stared at her. "What are you telling me? That it was you who killed Iida?" she whispered.

Kaede nodded. "Takeo took his head, but he was already

dead. I did what you told me. He was going to rape me."

Shizuka grasped her hands. "Never let anyone know that! Not one of these warriors, not even Arai, would let you live."

"I feel no guilt or remorse," Kaede said. "I never did a less shameful deed. Not only did I protect myself but the deaths of many were avenged: Lord Shigeru; my kinswoman, Lady Maruyama, and her daughter; and all the other innocent people whom Iida tortured and murdered."

"Nevertheless, if this became generally known, you would be punished for it. Men would think the world turned upside down if women start taking up arms and seeking revenge."

"My world is already turned upside down," Kaede said. "Still, I must go and see Lord Arai. Bring me—" She broke off and laughed. "I was going to say, 'bring me some clothes,' but I have none. I have nothing!"

"You have a horse," Shizuka replied. "Takeo left the gray for you."

"He left me Raku?" Kaede smiled, a true smile that illuminated her face. She stared into the distance, her eyes dark and thoughtful.

"Lady?" Shizuka touched her on the shoulder.

"Comb out my hair and send a message to Lord Arai to say I will visit him directly."

It was almost completely dark by the time they left the women's rooms and went toward the main guest rooms where Arai and his men were staying. Lights gleamed from the temple, and farther up the slope, beneath the trees, men stood with flaring torches around Lord Shigeru's grave. Even at this hour people came to visit it, bringing incense and offerings, placing lamps and candles on the ground around the stone, seeking the help of the dead man who every day became more of a god to them.

He sleeps beneath a covering of flame, Kaede thought, herself praying silently to Shigeru's spirit for guidance while she pondered what she should say to Arai. She was the heir to both Shirakawa and Maruyama; she knew Arai would be seeking some strong alliance with her, probably some marriage that would bind her into the power he was amassing. They had spoken a few times during her stay at Inuyama, and again on the journey, but Arai's attention had been taken up with securing the countryside and his strategies for the future. He had not shared these with her, beyond expressing his desire for the Otori marriage to take place. Once—a lifetime ago, it seemed now—she had wanted to be more than a pawn in the hands of the warriors who commanded her fate. Now, with the newfound strength that the icy sleep had given her, she resolved again to take control of her life. *I need time,* she thought. *I must do nothing rashly. I must go home before I make any decisions.*

One of Arai's men—she remembered his name was Niwa—greeted her at the veranda's edge and led her to the doorway. The shutters all stood open. Arai sat at the end of the room, three of his men next to him. Niwa spoke her name and the warlord looked up at her. For a moment they studied each other. She held his gaze and felt power's strong pulse in her veins. Then she dropped to her knees and bowed to him, resenting the gesture yet knowing she had to appear to submit.

He returned her bow, and they both sat up at the same time. Kaede felt his eyes on her. She raised her head and gave him the same unflinching look. He could not meet it. Her heart was pounding at her audacity. In the past she had both liked and trusted the man in front of her. Now she saw changes in his face. The lines had deepened around his mouth and eyes. He had been both pragmatic and flexible, but now he was in the grip of his intense desire for power.

Not far from her parents' home, the Shirakawa flowed through vast limestone caves where the water had formed pillars and statues. As a child she was taken there every year to worship the goddess who lived within one of these pillars under the mountain. The statue had a fluid, living shape, as though the spirit that dwelt within were trying to break out from beneath the covering of lime. She thought of that stone covering now. Was power a limy river calcifying those who dared to swim in it?

Arai's physical size and strength made her quail inwardly, reminding her of that moment of helplessness in Iida's arms, of the strength of men who could force women in any way they wanted. *Never let them use that strength,* came the thought, and then: *Always be armed.* A taste came into her mouth, as sweet as persimmon, as strong as blood: the knowledge and taste of power. Was this what drove men to clash endlessly with each other, to enslave and destroy each other? Why should a woman not have that too?

She stared at the places on Arai's body where the needle

and the knife had pierced Iida, had opened him up to the world he'd tried to dominate and let his life's blood leak away. *I must never forget it,* she told herself. *Men also can be killed by women. I killed the most powerful warlord in the Three Countries.*

All her upbringing had taught her to defer to men, to submit to their will and their greater intelligence. Her heart was beating so strongly, she thought she might faint. She breathed deeply, using the skills Shizuka had taught her, and felt the blood settle in her veins.

"Lord Arai, tomorrow I will leave for Shirakawa. I would be very grateful if you will provide men to escort me home."

"I would prefer you to stay in the East," he said, slowly. "But that is not what I want to talk to you about first." His eyes narrowed as he stared at her. "Otori's disappearance: Can you shed any light on this extraordinary occurrence? I believe I have established my right to power. I was already in alliance with Shigeru. How can young Otori ignore all obligations to me and to his dead father? How can he disobey and walk away? And where has he gone? My men have been searching the district all day, as far as Yamagata. He's completely vanished."

"I do not know where he is," she replied.

"I'm told he spoke to you last night before he left."

"Yes," she said simply.

"He must have explained to you at least—"

"He was bound by other obligations." Kaede felt sorrow build within her as she spoke. "He did not intend to insult you." Indeed, she could not remember Takeo mentioning Arai to her, but she did not say this.

"Obligations to the so-called Tribe?" Arai had been controlling his anger, but now it burst fresh into his voice, into his eyes. He moved his head slightly, and she guessed he was looking past her to where Shizuka knelt in the shadows on the veranda. "What do you know of them?"

"Very little," she replied. "It was with their help that Lord Takeo climbed into Inuyama. I suppose we are all in their debt in that respect."

Speaking Takeo's name made her shiver. She recalled the feel of his body against hers, at that moment when they both expected to die. Her eyes darkened, her face softened. Arai was aware of it, without knowing the reason, and when he spoke again she heard something else in his voice besides rage.

"Another marriage can be arranged for you. There are

other young men of the Otori, cousins to Shigeru. I will send envoys to Hagi."

"I am in mourning for Lord Shigeru," she replied. "I cannot consider marriage to anyone. I will go home and recover from my grief." *Will anyone ever want to marry me, knowing my reputation?* she wondered, and could not help following with the thought: *Takeo did not die.* She had thought Arai would argue further, but after a moment he concurred.

"Maybe it's best that you go to your parents. I will send for you when I return to Inuyama. We will discuss your marriage then."

"Will you make Inuyama your capital?"

"Yes. I intend to rebuild the castle." In the flickering light his face was set and brooding. Kaede said nothing. He spoke again abruptly. "But to return to the Tribe: I had not realized how strong their influence must be. To make Takeo walk away from such a marriage, such an inheritance, and then to conceal him completely . . . to tell you the truth, I had no idea what I was dealing with." He glanced again toward Shizuka.

He will kill her, she thought. *It's more than just anger at Takeo's disobedience: His self-esteem has been deeply wounded too. He must suspect*

Shizuka has been spying on him for years. She wondered what happened to the love and desire that had existed between them. Had it all dissolved overnight? Did the years of service, the trust, and loyalty, all come to nothing?

"I shall make it my business to find out about them," he went on, almost as if he were speaking to himself. "There must be people who know, who will talk. I cannot let such an organization exist. They will undermine my power as the white ant chews through wood."

Kaede said, "I believe it was you who sent Muto Shizuka to me, to protect me. I owe my life to that protection. And I believe I kept faith with you in Noguchi Castle. Strong bonds exist between us and they shall be unbroken. Whoever I marry will swear allegiance to you. Shizuka will remain in my service and will come with me to my parents' home."

He looked at her then, and again she met his gaze with ice in her eyes. "It's barely thirteen months since I killed a man for your sake," he said. "You were hardly more than a child. You have changed. . . ."

"I have been made to grow up," she replied. She made an effort not to think of her borrowed robe, her complete lack of possessions. *I am the heir to a great domain,* she told herself.

She continued to hold his eyes until he reluctantly inclined his head.

"Very well. I will send men with you to Shirakawa, and you may take the Muto woman."

"Lord Arai." Only then did she drop her eyes and bow.

Arai called to Niwa to make arrangements for the following day, and Kaede bade him good night, speaking with great deference. She felt she had come out of the encounter well; she could afford to pretend that all power lay on his side.

She returned to the women's rooms with Shizuka, both of them silent. The old woman had already spread out the beds, and now she brought sleeping garments for them before helping Shizuka undress Kaede. Wishing them good night, she retired to the adjoining room.

Shizuka's face was pale and her demeanor more subdued than Kaede had ever known it. She touched Kaede's hand and whispered, "Thank you," but said nothing else. When they were both lying beneath the cotton quilts, as mosquitoes whined around their heads and moths fluttered against the lamps, Kaede could feel the other woman's body rigid next to hers, and knew Shizuka was struggling with grief. Yet, she did not cry.

Kaede reached out and put her arms around Shizuka, holding her closely without speaking. She shared the same deep sorrow but no tears came to her eyes. She would allow nothing to weaken the power that was coming to life within her.

2

The next morning palanquins and an escort had been prepared for the women. They left as soon as the sun was up. Remembering the advice of her kinswoman Lady Maruyama, Kaede stepped delicately into the palanquin as though she were as frail and powerless as most women, but she made sure the grooms brought Takeo's horse from the stable and, once they were on the road, she opened the waxed paper curtains so she could look out.

The swaying movement was intolerable to her, and even being able to see did not prevent sickness from coming over her. At the first rest stop, at Yamagata, she was so dizzy she could hardly walk. She could not bear to look at food, and when she drank a little tea it made her vomit immediately. Her body's weakness infuriated her, seeming to undermine her newly discovered feeling of power. Shizuka led her to a small room in the rest house, bathed her face with cold water, and made her lie down for a while. The sickness passed as quickly as it had come, and she was able to drink some red-bean soup and a bowl of tea.

The sight of the black palanquin, however, made her feel queasy again. "Bring me the horse," she said. "I will ride."

The groom lifted her onto Raku's back, and Shizuka mounted nimbly behind her, and so they rode for the rest of the morning, saying little, each wrapped in her own thoughts but taking comfort from the other's closeness.

After they left Yamagata the road began to climb steeply. In places it was stepped with huge, flat stones. There were already signs of autumn, though the sky was clear blue and the air warm. Beech, sumac, and maple were beginning to turn gold and vermilion. Strings of wild geese flew high above them. The forest deepened, still and airless. The horse walked delicately, its head low as it picked its way up the steps. The men were alert and uneasy. Since the overthrow of Iida and the Tohan, the countryside was filled with masterless men of all ranks who resorted to banditry rather than swear new allegiances.

The horse was strong and fit. Despite the heat and the climb, its coat was hardly darkened with sweat when they stopped again at a small rest house at the top of the pass. It was a little past midday. The horses were led away to be fed and watered, the men retired to the shade trees around the well, and an old woman spread mattresses on the floor of a matted room so Kaede might rest for an hour or two.

Kaede lay down, thankful to be able to stretch out. The light in the room was dim and green. Huge cedars shut out most of the glare. In the distance she could hear the cool trickle of the spring, and voices; the men talking quietly, occasionally a ripple of laughter, Shizuka chatting to someone in the kitchen. At first Shizuka's voice was bright and gossipy, and Kaede was glad that she seemed to be recovering her spirits, but then it went low, and the person to whom she was speaking responded in the same vein. Kaede could no longer make out anything they said.

After a while the conversation ceased. Shizuka came quietly into the room and lay down next to Kaede.

"Who were you talking to?"

Shizuka turned her head so she could speak directly into Kaede's ear. "A cousin of mine works here."

"You have cousins everywhere."

"That's how it is with the Tribe."

Kaede was silent for a moment. Then she said, "Don't other people suspect who you are and want to . . ."

"Want to what?"

"Well, get rid of you."

Shizuka laughed. "No one dares. *We* have infinitely more ways of getting rid of *them.* And no one ever knows anything about us for sure. They have their suspicions. But you may have noticed, both my uncle Kenji and I can appear in many different guises. The Tribe are hard to recognize, in addition to possessing many other arts."

"Will you tell me more about them?" Kaede was fascinated by this world that lay in the shadows of the world she knew.

"I can tell you a little. Not everything. Later, when we cannot be overheard."

From outside a crow called harshly.

Shizuka said, "I learned two things from my cousin. One is that Takeo has not left Yamagata. Arai has search parties out and guards on the highway. They will be concealing him within the town."

The crow cried again. *Aah! Aah!*

I might have passed his hiding place today, Kaede thought. After a long moment she said, "What was the second thing?"

"An accident may occur on the road."

"What sort of accident?"

"To me. It seems Arai does want to get rid of me, as you put it. But it is planned to look like an accident, a brigand attack, something like that. He cannot bear that I should live, but he does not wish to offend you outright."

"You must leave." Kaede's voice rose with urgency. "As long as you are with me, he knows where to find you."

"Shush," Shizuka warned. "I'm only telling you so you won't do anything foolish."

"What would be foolish?"

"To use your knife, to try to defend me."

"I would do that," Kaede said.

"I know. But you must keep your boldness and those skills hidden. Someone is traveling with us who will protect me. More than one probably. Leave the fighting to them."

"Who is it?"

"If my lady can guess, I'll give her a present!" Shizuka said lightly.

"What happened to your broken heart?" Kaede asked, curious.

"I mended it with rage," Shizuka replied. Then she spoke more seriously. "I may never love a man as much again. But I have done nothing shameful. I am not the one who has acted with dishonor. Before, I was bound to him, a hostage to him. In cutting me off from him, he has set me free."

"You should leave me," Kaede said again.

"How can I leave you now? You need me more than ever."

Kaede lay still. "Why more than ever now?"

"Lady, you must know. Your bleeding is late, your face is softer, your hair thicker. The sickness, followed by hunger . . ." Shizuka's voice was soft, filled with pity.

Kaede's heart began to race. The knowledge lay beneath her skin, but she could not bring herself to face it.

"What will I do?"

"Whose child is it? Not Iida's?"

"I killed Iida before he could rape me. If it's true there is a child, it can only be Takeo's."

"When?" Shizuka whispered.

"The night Iida died. Takeo came to my room. We both expected to die."

Shizuka breathed out. "I sometimes think he is touched by madness."

"Not madness. Bewitchment, maybe," Kaede said. "It's as if we were both under a spell ever since we met in Tsuwano."

"Well, my uncle and I are partly to blame for that. We should never have brought you together."

"There was nothing you or anyone could have done to prevent it," Kaede said. Despite herself, a quiet intimation of joy stirred within her.

"If it were Iida's child, I would know what to do," Shizuka said. "I would not hesitate. There are things I can give you that will get rid of it. But Takeo's child is my own kin, my own blood."

Kaede said nothing. *The child may inherit Takeo's gifts,* she was thinking, *those gifts that make him valuable. Everyone wanted to use him for some purpose of their own. But I love him for himself alone. I will never get rid of his child. And I will never let the Tribe take it from me. But would Shizuka try? Would she so betray me?*

She was silent for so long, Shizuka sat up to see if she

had fallen asleep. But Kaede's eyes were open, staring at the green light beyond the doorway.

"How long will the sickness last?" Kaede said.

"Not long. And you will not show for three or four months."

"You know about these things. You said you have two sons?"

"Yes. Arai's children."

"Where are they?"

"With my grandparents. He does not know where they are."

"Hasn't he acknowledged them?"

"He was interested enough in them until he married and had a son by his legal wife," Shizuka said. "Then, since my sons are older, he began to see them as a threat to his heir. I realized what he was thinking and took them away to a hidden village the Muto family have. He must never know where they are."

Kaede shivered despite the heat. "You think he would harm them?"

"It would not be the first time a lord, a warrior, had done so," Shizuka replied bitterly.

"I am afraid of my father," Kaede said. "What will he do to me?"

Shizuka whispered, "Suppose Lord Shigeru, fearing Iida's treachery, insisted on a secret marriage at Terayama, the day we visited the temple. Your kinswoman, Lady Maruyama, and her companion, Sachie, were the witnesses, but they did not live."

"I cannot lie to the world in that way," Kaede began.

Shizuka hushed her. "You do not need to say anything. It has all been hidden. You are following your late husband's wishes. I will let it be known, as if inadvertently. You'll see how these men can't keep a secret among themselves."

"What about documents, proof?"

"They were lost when Inuyama fell, along with everything else. The child will be Shigeru's. If it is a boy, it will be the heir to the Otori."

"That is too far in the future to think about," Kaede said quickly. "Don't tempt fate." For Shigeru's real unborn child came into her mind, the one that had perished silently within its mother's body in the waters of the river at Inuyama. She prayed that its ghost would not be jealous, she prayed her own child would live.

Before the end of the week the sickness had eased a little. Kaede's breasts swelled, her nipples ached, and she became suddenly, urgently hungry at unexpected times, but otherwise she began to feel well, better than she had ever felt in her life. Her senses were heightened almost as if the child shared its gifts with her. She noted with amazement how Shizuka's secret information spread through the men as, one by one, they began to address her as Lady Otori, in lowered voices and with averted eyes. The pretense made her uneasy, but she went along with it, not knowing what else to do.

She studied the men carefully, trying to discern which was the member of the Tribe who would protect Shizuka when the moment came. Shizuka had regained her cheerfulness and laughed and joked with them all equally, and they all responded, with different emotions ranging from appreciation to desire, but not one of them seemed to be particularly vigilant.

Because they rarely looked at Kaede directly, they would have been surprised at how well she came to know them. She could distinguish each of them in the dark by his tread or his voice, sometimes even by his smell. She gave them names: Scar, Squint, Silent, Long Arm.

Long Arm's smell was of the hot spiced oil that the men used to flavor their rice. His voice was low, roughly accented. He had a look about him that suggested insolence to her, a sort of irony that annoyed her. He was of medium build, with a high forehead and eyes that bulged a little and were so black he seemed to have no pupils. He had a habit of screwing them up and then sniffing with a flick of his head. His arms were abnormally long and his hands big. If anyone were going to murder a woman, Kaede thought, it would be him.

In the second week a sudden storm delayed them in a small village. Confined by the rain to the narrow, uncomfortable room, Kaede was restless. She was tormented by thoughts of her mother. When she sought her in her mind she met nothing but darkness. She tried to recall her face but could not. Nor could she summon up her sisters' appearance. The youngest would be almost nine. If her mother, as she feared, was dead, she would have to take her place, be a mother to her sisters, run the household, overseeing the cooking, cleaning, weaving, and sewing that were the year-round chores of women, taught to girls by their mothers and aunts and grandmothers. She knew nothing of such things. When she had been a hostage she had been neglected by the

Noguchi family. They had taught her so little; all she had learned was how to survive on her own in the castle while she ran around like a maid, waiting on the armed men. Well, she would have to learn these practical skills. The child gave her feelings and instincts she had not known before: the instinct to take care of her people. She thought of the Shirakawa retainers, men like Shoji Kiyoshi and Amano Tenzo, who had come with her father when he had visited her at Noguchi Castle, and the servants of the house, like Ayame, whom she had missed almost as much as her mother when she had been taken away at seven years old. Was Ayame still alive? Would she still remember the girl she had looked after? Kaede was returning, ostensibly married and widowed, another man dead on her account, and she was pregnant. What would her welcome be at her parents' home?

The delay irritated the men too. She knew they were anxious to be done with this tiresome duty, impatient to return to the battles that were their real work, their life. They wanted to be part of Arai's victories over the Tohan in the East, not far away from the action in the West, looking after women.

Arai was only one of them, she thought wonderingly.

How had he suddenly become so powerful? What did he have that made these men, each of them adult, physically strong, want to follow and obey him? She remembered again his swift ruthlessness when he had cut the throat of the guard who had attacked her in Noguchi Castle. He would not hesitate to kill any one of these men in the same way. Yet, it was not fear that made them obey him. Was it a sort of trust in that ruthlessness, in that willingness to act immediately, whether the act was right or wrong? Would they ever trust a woman in that way? Could she command men as he did? Would warriors like Shoji and Amano obey her?

The rain stopped and they moved on. The storm had cleared the last of the humidity and the days that followed were brilliant, the sky huge and blue above the mountain peaks where every day the maples showed more red. The nights grew cooler, already with a hint of the frost to come.

The journey wound on and the days became long and tiring. Finally one morning Shizuka said, "This is the last pass. Tomorrow we will be at Shirakawa."

They were descending a steep path, so densely carpeted with pine needles the horses' feet made no noise. Shizuka was walking alongside Raku while Kaede rode. Beneath the pines and cedars it was dark, but a little ahead of them the sun slanted through a bamboo grove, casting a dappled, greenish light.

"Have you been on this road before?" Kaede asked.

"Many times. The first time was years ago. I was sent to Kumamoto to work for the Arai family when I was younger than you are now. The old lord was still alive then. He kept his sons under an iron rule, but the oldest—Daiichi is his given name—still found ways to take the maids to bed. I resisted him for a long time; it's not easy, as you know, for girls living in castles. I was determined he would not forget me as quickly as he forgot most of them. And naturally I was also under instructions from my family, the Muto."

"So you were spying on him all that time," Kaede murmured.

"Certain people were interested in the Arai allegiances, particularly in Daiichi, before he went to the Noguchi."

"*Certain people* meaning Iida?"

"Of course. It was part of the settlement with the Seishuu clan after Yaegahara. Arai was reluctant to serve Noguchi. He disliked Iida and thought Noguchi a traitor, but he was compelled to obey."

"You worked for Iida?"

"You know who I work for," Shizuka said quietly. "Always in the first instance for the Muto family, for the Tribe. Iida employed many of the Muto at that time."

"I'll never understand it," Kaede said. The alliances of her class were complex enough, with new ones being formed through marriage, old ones maintained by hostages, allegiances being broken by sudden insults or feuds or sheer opportunism. Yet, these seemed straightforward compared to the intrigues of the Tribe. The unpleasant thought that Shizuka only stayed with her on orders from the Muto family came to her again.

"Are you spying on me?"

Shizuka made a sign with her hand to silence her. The men rode ahead and behind, out of earshot, Kaede thought.

"Are you?"

Shizuka put her hand on the horse's shoulder. Kaede looked down on the back of her head, the white nape of her neck beneath the dark hair. Her head was turned away so Kaede could not see her face. Shizuka kept pace with the horse as it stepped down the slope, swinging its haunches to keep its balance. Kaede leaned forward and tried to speak quietly. "Tell me."

Then the horse startled and plunged suddenly. Kaede's forward movement turned into a sudden downward dive.

I'm going to fall, she thought in amazement, and the ground rushed up toward her as she and Shizuka fell together.

The horse was jumping sideways as it tried not to step on them. Kaede was aware of more confusion, a greater danger.

"Shizuka!" she cried.

"Keep down," the girl replied, and pushed her to the ground, but Kaede struggled to look.

There were men on the path ahead, two of them; wild bandits by the look of them, with drawn swords. She felt for her knife, longed for a sword or a pole at least, remembered her promise, all in a split second before she heard the thrum of a bowstring. An arrow flew past the horse's ears, making it jump and buck again.

There was a brief cry and one man fell at her feet, blood streaming from where the arrow had pierced his neck.

The second man faltered for a moment. The horse plunged sideways, knocking him off balance. He swung his sword in a desperate sideways slice at Shizuka, then Long Arm was on him, coming up under the blow with almost supernatural speed, his sword's tip seeming to find its own way into the man's throat.

The men in front turned and ran back, those behind came milling forward. Shizuka had caught the horse by the bridle and was calming it.

Long Arm helped Kaede to her feet. "Don't be alarmed, Lady Otori," he said in his rough accent, the smell of pepper oil strong on his breath. "They were just brigands."

Just brigands? Kaede thought. They had died so suddenly and with so much blood. *Brigands, maybe, but in whose pay?*

The men took their weapons and drew lots for them, then threw the bodies into the undergrowth. It was impossible to tell if any one of them had anticipated the attack or was disappointed in its failure. They seemed to show more deference to Long Arm, and she realized they were impressed by the swiftness of his reaction and his fighting skills, but otherwise they acted as if it was a normal occurrence, one of the hazards of travel. One or two of them joked with Shizuka that the bandits wanted her as a wife, and she answered in the same vein, adding that the forest was full of such desperate men, but even a bandit had more chance with her than any of the escort.

"I would never have picked your defender," Kaede said later. "In fact, quite the opposite. He was the one I suspected would kill you with those big hands of his."

Shizuka laughed. "He's quite a clever fellow, and a ruthless fighter. It's easy to misjudge or underestimate him. You were not the only person surprised by him. Were you afraid at that moment?"

Kaede tried to remember. "No, mainly because there was no time. I wished I had a sword."

Shizuka said, "You have the gift of courage."

"It's not true. I am often afraid."

"No one would ever guess," Shizuka murmured. They had come to an inn in a small town on the border of the Shirakawa domain. Kaede had been able to bathe in the hot spring, and she was now in her night attire, waiting for the evening meal to be brought. Her welcome at the inn had been perfunctory, and the town itself made her uneasy. There seemed to be little food, and the people were sullen and dispirited.

She was bruised down one side from the fall, and she feared for the child. She was also nervous about meeting her father. Would he believe she had married Lord Otori? She could not imagine his fury if he discovered the truth.

"I don't feel very brave at the moment," she confessed.

Shizuka said, "I'll massage your head. You look exhausted."

But even as she leaned back and enjoyed the feeling of the girl's fingers against her scalp, Kaede's misgivings increased. She remembered what they had been talking about at the moment of the attack.

"You will be home tomorrow," Shizuka said, feeling her tension. "The journey is nearly over."

"Shizuka, answer me truthfully: What's the real reason you stay with me? Is it to spy on me? Who employs the Muto now?"

"No one employs us at the moment. Iida's downfall has thrown the whole of the Three Countries into confusion. Arai is saying he will wipe out the Tribe. We don't know yet if he is serious or if he will come to his senses and work with us. In the meantime my uncle, Kenji, who admires Lady Shirakawa greatly, wants to be kept informed of her welfare and her intentions."

And of my child, Kaede thought, but did not speak it. Instead she asked, "My intentions?"

"You are heir to one of the richest and most powerful

domains in the West, Maruyama, as well as to your own estate of Shirakawa. Whoever you marry will become a key player in the future of the Three Countries. At the moment everyone assumes you will maintain the alliance with Arai, strengthening his position in the West while he settles the Otori question; your destiny is closely linked with the Otori clan and with the Middle Country too."

"I may marry no one," Kaede said, half to herself. *And in that case,* she was thinking, *why should I not become a key player myself?*

3

The sounds of the temple at Terayama, the midnight bell, the chanting of the monks, faded from my hearing as I followed the two masters, Kikuta Kotaro and Muto Kenji, down a lonely path, steep and overgrown, alongside the stream. We went swiftly, the noise of the tumbling water hiding our footsteps. We said little and we saw no one.

By the time we came to Yamagata, it was nearly dawn and the first cocks were crowing. The streets of the town were deserted, though the curfew was lifted and the Tohan no longer there to patrol them. We came to a merchant's house in the middle of the town, not far from the inn where we had stayed during the Festival of the Dead. I already knew the street from when I had explored the town at night. It seemed a lifetime ago.

Kenji's daughter, Yuki, opened the gate as though she had been waiting for us all night, even though we came so silently that not a dog barked. She said nothing, but I caught the intensity in the look she gave me. Her face, her vivid eyes, her graceful, muscular body, brought back all too clearly the terrible events at Inuyama the night Shigeru died. I had half-expected to see her at Terayama, for it was she who had traveled day and night to take Shigeru's head to the temple and break the news of his death. There were many things I would have liked to have questioned her about: her journey, the uprising at Yamagata, the overthrow of the Tohan. As her father and the Kikuta master went ahead into the house, I lingered a little so that she and I stepped up onto the veranda together. A low light was burning by the doorway.

She said, "I did not expect to see you alive again."

"I did not expect to live." Remembering her skill and her ruthlessness, I added, "I owe you a huge debt. I can never repay you."

She smiled. "I was repaying debts of my own. You owe me nothing. But I hope we will be friends."

The word did not seem strong enough to describe what we already were. She had brought Shigeru's sword, Jato, to me and had helped me in his rescue and revenge: the most important and most desperate acts of my life. I was filled with gratitude for her, mingled with admiration.

She disappeared for a moment and came back with water. I washed my feet, listening to the two masters talking within the house. They planned to rest for a few hours, then I would travel on with Kotaro. I shook my head wearily. I was tired of listening.

"Come," she said, and led me into the center of the house, where, as in Inuyama, there was a concealed room as narrow as an eel's bed.

"Am I a prisoner again?" I said, looking around at the windowless walls.

"No, it's only for your own safety, to rest for a few hours. Then you will travel on."

"I know; I heard."

"Of course," she said. "I forgot: You hear everything."

"Too much," I said, sitting down on the mattress that was already spread out on the floor.

"Gifts are hard. But it's better to have them than not. I'll get you some food, and tea is ready."

She came back in a few moments. I drank the tea but could not face food. "There's no hot water to bathe," she said. "I'm sorry."

"I'll live." Twice already she had bathed me. Once here, in Yamagata, when I did not know who she was and she had scrubbed my back and massaged my temples, and then again in Inuyama, when I could barely walk. The memory came flooding over me. Her gaze met mine, and I knew she was thinking of the same thing. Then she looked away and said quietly, "I'll leave you to sleep."

I placed my knife close to the mattress and slid beneath the quilt without bothering to undress. I thought of what Yuki had said about gifts. I did not think I would ever be as happy again as I had been in the village where I was born, Mino—but in Mino I was a child, and now the village was destroyed, my family all dead. I knew I must not dwell on the past. I had agreed to come to the Tribe. It was because of my gifts that they wanted me so badly, and it was only with the Tribe that I would learn to develop and control the skills I had been given.

I thought of Kaede, whom I had left sleeping at Terayama. Hopelessness came over me, followed by resignation. I would never see her again. I would have to forget her. Slowly the town started to wake around me. Finally, as the light brightened beyond the doors, I slept.

I woke suddenly to the sound of men and horses in the street beyond the walls of the house. The light in the room had changed, as though the sun had crossed above the roof, but I had no idea how long I'd slept. A man was shouting and in reply a woman was complaining, growing angry. I caught the gist of the words. The men were Arai's, going from house to house, looking for me.

I pushed back the quilt and felt for the knife. As I picked it up the door slid open and Kenji came silently into the room. The false wall was locked into place behind him. He looked at me briefly, shook his head, and sat down cross-legged on the floor in the tiny space between the mattress and the wall.

I recognized the voices; the men had been at Terayama with Arai. I heard Yuki calming the angry woman down, offering the men a drink.

"We're all on the same side now," she said, and laughed.

"Do you think if Otori Takeo were here we'd be able to hide him?"

The men drank quickly and left. As their footsteps died away Kenji snorted through his nose and gave me one of his disparaging looks. "No one can pretend not to have heard of you in Yamagata," he said. "Shigeru's death made him a god; Iida's has turned you into a hero. It's a story the people are wild about." He sniffed and added, "Don't let it go to your head. It's extremely annoying. Now Arai's mounted a full-scale search for you. He's taking your disappearance as a personal insult. Luckily your face is not too well known here, but we'll have to disguise you." He studied my features, frowning. "That Otori look . . . you'll have to conceal it."

He was interrupted by a sound outside as the wall was lifted away. Kikuta Kotaro came in, followed by Akio, the young man who had been one of my captors in Inuyama. Yuki stepped after them, bringing tea.

The Kikuta master gave me a nod as I bowed to him. "Akio has been out in the town, listening to the news."

Akio dropped to his knees before Kenji and inclined his head slightly to me. I responded in the same way. When he and the other Tribe members had kidnapped me in Inuyama, they had been doing their best to restrain me without hurting me. I had been fighting in earnest. I had wanted to kill him. I had cut him. I could see now that his left hand still bore a half-healed scar, red and inflamed. We had hardly spoken before; he had reprimanded me for my lack of manners and had accused me of breaking every rule of the Tribe. There had been little goodwill between us. Now when our eyes met I felt his deep hostility.

Akio said, "It seems Lord Arai is furious that this person left without permission and refused a marriage that the lord desired. Lord Arai has issued orders for this person's arrest, and he intends to investigate the organization known as the Tribe, which he considers illegal and undesirable." He bowed again to Kotaro and said stiffly, "I'm sorry, but I do not know what this person's name is to be."

The master nodded and stroked his chin, saying nothing. We had talked about names before and he had told me to continue using Takeo—though, as he said, it had never been a Tribe name. Was I to take the family name of Kikuta now? And what would my given name be? I did not want to give up Takeo, the name Shigeru had given me, but if I was no longer to be one of the Otori, what right did I have to it?

"Arai is offering rewards for information," Yuki said, placing a bowl of tea on the matting in front of each of us.

"No one in Yamagata will dare to volunteer information," Akio said. "They'll be dealt with if they do!"

"It's what I was afraid of," Kotaro said to Kenji. "Arai has had no real dealings with us, and now he fears our power."

"Should we eliminate him?" Akio said eagerly. "We—"

Kotaro made a movement with his hand, and the young man bowed again and fell silent.

"With Iida gone, there is already a lack of stability. If Arai should perish, too, who knows what anarchy would break out?"

Kenji said, "I don't see Arai as any great danger. Threats and bluster, perhaps, but no more than that in the long run. As things have turned out now, he is our best hope for peace." He glanced at me. "That's what we desire above all. We need some degree of order for our work to flourish."

"Arai will return to Inuyama and make that his capital," Yuki said. "It is easier to defend and more central than Kumamoto, and he has claimed all Iida's lands by right of conquest."

"Unh," Kotaro grunted. He turned to me. "I had planned for you to return to Inuyama with me. I have matters to attend to there for the next few weeks, and you would have begun your training there. However, it may be better if you remain here for a few days. We will then take you north beyond the Middle Country, to another of the Kikuta houses, where no one has heard of Otori Takeo—where you will start a new life. Do you know how to juggle?"

I shook my head.

"You have a week to learn. Akio will teach you. Yuki and some of the other actors will accompany you. I will meet you in Matsue."

I bowed, saying nothing. I looked from under my lowered eyelids at Akio. He was staring downward, frowning, the line deep between his eyes. He was only three or four years older than I was, but at that moment it was possible to see what he would be like as an old man. So he was a juggler. I was sorry I had cut his clever juggler's hand, but I thought my actions perfectly justified. Still, the fight lay between us, along with other feelings, unresolved, festering.

Kotaro said, "Kenji, your association with Lord Shigeru has singled you out in this affair. Too many people know that this is your main place of residence. Arai will certainly have you arrested if you stay here."

"I'll go to the mountains for a while," Kenji replied. "Visit the old people, spend some time with the children." He smiled, looking like my harmless old teacher again.

"Excuse me, but what is this person to be called?" Akio said.

"He can take a name as an actor for the time being," Kotaro said. "What his Tribe name is depends—"

There was some meaning behind his words that I did not understand, but Akio all too clearly did. "His father renounced the Tribe!" he burst out. "He turned his back on us!"

"But his son has returned, with all the gifts of the Kikuta," the master replied. "However, for now, in everything you are his senior. Takeo, you will submit to Akio and learn from him."

A smile played on his lips. I think he knew how hard that would be for me. Kenji's face was rueful, as if he also could foresee trouble.

"Akio has many skills," Kotaro went on. "You are to master them." He waited for my acceptance, then told Akio and Yuki to leave. Yuki refilled the tea bowls before she left, and the two older men drank noisily. I could smell food cooking. It seemed like days since I'd last eaten. I was sorry I had not accepted Yuki's offer of food the previous night; I was faint with hunger.

Kotaro said, "I told you I was first cousin to your father. I did not tell you that he was older than me and would have become master at our grandfather's death. Akio is my nephew and my heir. Your return raises questions of inheritance and seniority. How we deal with them depends on your conduct in the next few months."

It took me a couple of moments to grasp his meaning. "Akio was brought up in the Tribe," I said slowly. "He knows everything I don't know. There must be many others like that. I've no wish to take his or anyone else's place."

"There are many," Kotaro replied, "and all of them more obedient, better trained, and more deserving than you. But none has the Kikuta gift of hearing to the extent that you have it, and no one else could have gone alone into Yamagata Castle as you did."

That episode seemed like something from a past life. I could hardly remember the impulse that had driven me to climb into the castle and release into death the Hidden who were encaged in baskets and hung from the castle walls, the first time I had killed. I wished I had never done it: If I had not drawn the Tribe's attention to myself so dramatically, maybe they would not have taken me before . . . before . . . I shook myself. There was no point in endlessly trying to unravel the threads that had woven Shigeru's death.

"However, now that I've said that," Kotaro continued, "you must know that I cannot treat you in any way differently from the others of your generation. I cannot have favorites. Whatever your skills, they are useless to us unless we also have your obedience. I don't have to remind you that you have already pledged this to me. You will stay here for a week. You must not go outside or let anyone know you are here. In that week you must learn enough to pass as a juggler. I will meet you at Matsue before winter. It's up to you to go through the training with complete obedience."

"Who knows when I will meet you again?" Kenji said, regarding me with his usual mixture of affection and exasperation. "My work with you is done," he went on. "I found you, taught you, kept you alive somehow, and brought you back to the Tribe. You'll find Akio tougher than I was." He grinned, showing the gaps between his teeth. "But Yuki will look after you."

There was something in the way he said it that made the

color rise in my face. We had done nothing, had not even touched each other, but something existed between us, and Kenji was aware of it.

Both masters were grinning as they stood up and embraced me. Kenji gave me a cuff round the head. "Do as you're told," he said. "And learn to juggle."

I wished Kenji and I could have spoken alone. There was so much still unresolved between us. Yet, maybe it was better that he should bid me farewell as though he truly were an affectionate teacher whom I had outgrown. Besides, as I was to learn, the Tribe do not waste time on the past and do not like to be confronted with it.

After they'd left, the room seemed gloomier than ever, airless and stuffy. I could hear through the house the sounds of their departure. The elaborate preparations, the long good-byes of most travelers, were not for them. Kenji and Kotaro just walked out the door, carrying everything they needed for the road in their hands: light bundles in wrapping cloths, a spare pair of sandals, some rice cakes flavored with salted plums. I thought about them and the roads they must have walked, tracing and retracing their way across the Three Countries and beyond, for all I knew, following the vast web the Tribe spun from village to village, town to town. Wherever they went they would find relatives; they would never be without shelter or protection.

I heard Yuki say she would walk with them to the bridge, and heard the woman who'd been angry with the soldiers reply.

"Take care of yourselves," the woman called after them. The footsteps faded down the street.

The room seemed even more depressing and lonely. I couldn't imagine being confined in it for a week. Almost without realizing what I was doing, I was already planning to get out. Not to escape: I was quite resigned to staying with the Tribe. Just to get out. Partly to look at Yamagata again by night, partly to see if I could.

Not long after, I heard someone approaching. The door slid back and a woman stepped in. She was carrying a tray of food: rice, pickles, a small piece of dried fish, a bowl of soup. She knelt, placing the tray on the floor.

"Here, eat, you must be hungry."

I was famished. The smell of the food made me dizzy. I fell on it like a wolf. She sat and watched me while I ate.

"So you're the one who's been causing my poor old

husband so much trouble," she remarked as I was polishing the bowl for the last grains of rice.

Kenji's wife. I shot a look at her and met her gaze. Her face was smooth, as pale as his, with the similarity that many long-married couples attain. Her hair was still thick and black, with just a few white hairs appearing at the center of her scalp. She was thickset and solid, a true townswoman with square, short-fingered, capable hands. The only thing I could remember Kenji saying about her was that she was a good cook, and indeed the food was delicious.

I told her so, and as the smile moved from her lips to her eyes I saw in an instant that she was Yuki's mother. Their eyes were the same shape, and when she smiled, the expression was the same.

"Who'd have thought that you'd have turned up after all these years," she went on, sounding garrulous and motherly. "I knew Isamu, your father, well. And no one knew anything about you until that incident with Shintaro. Imagine you hearing and outwitting the most dangerous assassin in the Three Countries! The Kikuta family were delighted to discover Isamu had left a son. We all were. And one with such talents too!"

I didn't reply. She seemed a harmless old woman—but then, Kenji had appeared a harmless old man. I felt in myself a faint echo of the mistrust I'd had when I first saw Kenji in the street in Hagi. I tried to study her without appearing to, and she stared openly at me. I felt she was challenging me in some way, but I had no intention of responding until I'd found out more about her and her skills.

"Who killed my father?" I said instead.

"No one's ever found out. It was years before we even knew for certain that he was dead. He'd found an isolated place to hide himself in."

"Was it someone from the Tribe?"

That made her laugh, which angered me. "Kenji said you trusted no one. It's good, but you can trust me."

"Like I could trust him," I muttered.

"Shigeru's scheme would have killed you," she said mildly. "It's important for the Kikuta, for the whole Tribe, to keep you alive. It's so rare these days to find such a wealth of talent."

I grunted at that, trying to discern some hidden meaning beneath her flattery. She poured tea, and I drank it at a gulp. My head ached from the stuffy room.

"You're tense," she said, taking the bowl from my hands

and placing it on the tray. She moved the tray to one side and came closer to me. Kneeling behind me, she began to massage my neck and shoulders. Her fingers were strong, pliant, and sensitive, all at the same time. She worked over my back and then, saying, "Close your eyes," began on my head. The sensation was exquisite. I almost groaned aloud. Her hands seemed to have a life of their own. I gave my head to them, feeling as though it were floating off my neck.

Then I heard the door slide. My eyes snapped open. I could still feel her fingers in my scalp, but I was alone in the room. A shiver ran down my spine. Kenji's wife might look harmless but her powers were probably as great as her husband's or her daughter's.

She'd also taken away my knife.

I was given the name of Minoru, but hardly anyone called me by it. When we were alone Yuki occasionally called me Takeo, letting the word form in her mouth as if she were granting herself a gift. Akio only said "you," and always in the form used when addressing inferiors. He was entitled to. He was my senior in years, training, and knowledge, and I'd been ordered to submit to him. It rankled, though: I hadn't realized how much I had become accustomed to being treated with respect as an Otori warrior and Shigeru's heir.

My training began that afternoon. I had not known that the muscles in my hands could ache so much. My right wrist was still weak from my first fight with Akio. By the end of the day it was throbbing again. We started with exercises to make the fingers deft and supple. Even with his damaged hand Akio was far faster and far more dexterous than me. We sat opposite each other and time and again he rapped my hands before I could move them.

He was so quick, I could not believe that I could not even see the movement. At first the rap was no more than a light tap, but as the afternoon turned to evening and we both grew tired and frustrated by my clumsiness, he began to hit me in earnest.

Yuki, who had come into the room to join us, said quietly, "If you bruise his hands, it will take longer."

"Maybe I should bruise his head," Akio muttered, and the next time, before I could move my hands away, he seized both in his right hand and, with the left, hit me on the cheek. It was a real blow, strong enough to make my eyes water.

"Not so bold without a knife," he said, releasing my hands and holding his own ready again.

Yuki said nothing. I could feel anger simmering inside me. It was outrageous to me that he should hit an Otori lord. The confined room, the deliberate teasing, Yuki's indifference—all combined to drive me toward loss of control. The next time Akio made the same move with opposite hands. The blow was even harder, making my neck snap back. My sight went black, then red. I felt the rage erupt just as it had with Kenji. I hurled myself at him.

It's been many years since I was seventeen, since the fury seized me and threw me beyond self-control. But I still recall the way the release felt, as though my animal self had been unleashed, and then I'd have no memory of what happened after that, just the blind feeling of not caring if I lived or died, of refusing to be forced or bullied any longer.

After the first moment of surprise, when I had my hands round Akio's throat, the two of them restrained me easily. Yuki did her trick of pressing into my neck, and as I began to black out, she hit me harder than I would have thought possible in the stomach. I doubled over, retching. Akio slid out from beneath me and pinioned my arms behind my back.

We sat on the matting, as close as lovers, breathing heavily. The whole episode had lasted no more than a minute. I couldn't believe Yuki had hit me so hard. I'd thought she would have been on my side. I stared at her with rancor in my heart.

"That's what you have to learn to control," she said calmly.

Akio released my arms and knelt in readiness. "Let's start again."

"Don't hit me in the face," I said.

"Yuki's right, it's best not to bruise your hands," he replied. "So be quicker."

I vowed inwardly I would not let him hit me again. The next time, though, I did not get close to rapping him; I moved head and hands away before he could touch me. Watching him, I began to sense the slightest intimation of movement. I finally managed to graze the surface of his knuckles. He said nothing, nodded as if satisfied, but barely, and we moved on to working with juggling balls.

So the hours went: passing the ball from one palm to the other, from palm to mat to palm. By the end of the second day I could juggle three balls in the ancient style; by the end of the third day, four. Akio still sometimes managed to catch me off guard and slap me, but mostly I learned to avoid it, in an elaborate dance of balls and hands.

By the end of the fourth day I was seeing balls behind my eyelids, and I was bored and restless beyond words. Some people, and I guessed Akio was one, work persistently at these skills because they are obsessed by them and by their desire to master them. I quickly realized I was not among them. I couldn't see the point to juggling. It didn't interest me. I was learning in the hardest of ways and for the worst of reasons: because I would be beaten if I did not. I submitted to Akio's harsh teaching because I had to, but I hated it, and I hated him. Twice more his goading led to the same outburst of fury, but just as I was learning to anticipate him, so he and Yuki came to know the signs, and were ready to restrain me before anyone got hurt.

That fourth night, once the house was silent and everyone slept, I decided to go exploring. I was bored, I could not sleep, I was longing to breathe some fresh air, but above all I wanted to see if I could. For obedience to the Tribe to make sense, I had to find out if I could be disobedient. Forced obedience seemed to have as little point as juggling. They might as well tie me up day and night like a dog, and I would growl and bite on command.

I knew the layout of the house. I had mapped it when I had nothing else to do but listen. I knew where everyone slept at night. Yuki and her mother were in a room at the back of the building, with two other women whom I had not seen, though I had heard them. One served in the shop, joking loudly with the customers in the local accent. Yuki addressed her as "Auntie." The other was more of a servant. She did the cleaning and most of the food preparation, always first up in the morning and the last to lie down at night. She spoke very little, in a low voice with a northern accent. Her name was Sadako. Everyone in the household bullied her cheerfully and took advantage of her; her replies were always quiet and deferential. I felt I knew these women, though I'd never set eyes on either of them.

Akio and the other men, three of them, slept in a loft in the roof space above the shop. Every night they took turns joining the guards at the back of the house. Akio had done it the night before, and I'd suffered for it, as sleeplessness added an extra edge to his teasing. Before the maid went to bed, while the lamps were still lit, I would hear one or other of the men help her close the doors and the outer shutters, the wooden panels sliding into place with a series of dull thumps that invariably set the dogs barking.

There were three dogs, each with its own distinctive voice. The same man fed them every night, whistling to them through his teeth in a particular way that I practiced when I was alone, thankful that no one else had the Kikuta gift of hearing.

The front doors of the house were barred at night, and the rear gates guarded, but one smaller door was left unbarred. It led into a narrow space between the house and the outer wall, at the end of which was the privy. I was escorted there three or four times a day. I'd been out in the yard after dark a couple of times, to bathe in the small bathhouse that stood in the backyard, between the end of the house and the gates. Though I was kept hidden, it was, as Yuki said, for my own safety. As far as I could tell, no one seriously expected me to try to escape: I was not under guard.

I lay for a long time, listening to the sounds of the house. I could hear the breathing of the women in the downstairs room, the men in the loft. Beyond the walls the town gradually quieted. I had gone into a state I recognized. I could not explain it, but it was as familiar to me as my own skin. I did not feel either fear or excitement. My brain switched off. I was all instinct, instinct and ears. Time altered and slowed. It did not matter how long it took to open the door of the concealed room. I knew I would do it eventually, and I would do it soundlessly. Just as I would get to the outer door silently.

I was standing by this outer door, aware of every noise around me, when I heard footsteps. Kenji's wife got up, crossed the room where she'd been sleeping, and went toward the concealed room. The door slid; a few seconds passed. She came out of the room and, a lamp in her hand, walked swiftly but not anxiously toward me. Briefly I thought of going invisible, but I knew there was no point. She would almost certainly be able to discern me, and if she couldn't she would raise the household.

Saying nothing, I jerked my head in the direction of the door that led to the privy and went back to the hidden room. As I passed her I was aware of her eyes on me. She didn't say anything, either, just nodded at me, but I felt she knew I was trying to get out.

The room was stuffier than ever. Sleep now seemed impossible. I was still deep within my state of silent instinct. I tried to discern her breathing, but could not hear it. Finally I convinced myself that she must be asleep again. I got up, slowly opened the door, and stepped out into the room. The lamp still burned. Kenji's wife sat there next to it. Her eyes were closed, but she opened them and saw me standing in front of her.

"Going to piss again?" she said in her deep voice.

"I can't sleep."

"Sit down. I'll make some tea." She got to her feet in one movement: Despite her age and size she was as lithe as a girl. She put her hand on my shoulder and pushed me gently down onto the matting.

"Don't run away!" she warned, mockery in her voice.

I sat, but I was not really thinking. I was still bent on getting outside. I heard the kettle hiss as she blew on the embers, heard the chink of iron and pottery. She came back with the tea, knelt to pour it, and handed me a bowl, which I leaned forward to take. The light glowed between us. As I took the bowl I looked into her eyes, saw the amusement and mockery in them, saw that she had been flattering me before: She did not really believe in my talents. Then her eyelids flickered and closed. I dropped the bowl, caught her as she swayed, and set her down, already deeply asleep, on the matting. In the lamplight the spilled tea steamed.

I should have been horrified, but I wasn't. I just felt the cold satisfaction that the skills of the Tribe bring with them. I was sorry that I hadn't thought of this before, but it had never occurred to me that I would have any power at all over the wife of the Muto master. I was mainly relieved that now nothing was going to stop me from getting outside.

As I slipped through the side door into the yard, I heard the dogs stir. I whistled to them, high and quiet so only they and I would hear. One came padding up to investigate me, tail wagging. In the way of all dogs, he liked me. I put out my hand. He laid his head on it. The moon was low in the sky, but it gave enough light to make his eyes shine yellow. We stared at each other for a few moments, then he yawned, showing his big white teeth, lay down at my feet, and slept.

Inside my head the thought niggled: *A dog is one thing, the Muto master's wife is quite another.* But I chose not to listen. I crouched down and stroked the dog's head a couple of times while I looked at the wall.

Of course, I had neither weapons nor tools. The overhang of the wall's roof was wide and so pitched that, without grapples, it was impossible to get a handhold. In the end I climbed onto the roof of the bathhouse and jumped across.

I went invisible, crept along the top of the wall away from the rear gate and the guards, and dropped into the street just before the corner. I stood against the wall for a few moments, listening. I heard the murmur of voices from the guards. The dogs were silent and the whole town seemed to sleep.

As I had done before, the night I climbed into Yamagata Castle, I worked my way from street to street, heading in a zigzag direction toward the river. The willow trees still stood beneath the setting moon. The branches moved gently in the autumn wind, the leaves already yellow, one or two floating down into the water.

I crouched in their shelter. I had no idea who controlled this town now: The lord whom Shigeru had visited, Iida's ally, had been overthrown along with the Tohan when the town erupted at the news of Shigeru's death, but presumably Arai had installed some kind of interim governor. I could not hear any sound of patrols. I stared at the castle, unable to make out if the heads of the Hidden whom I had released from torture into death had been removed or not. I could hardly believe my own memory: It was as if I had dreamed it or been told the story of someone else who had done it.

I was thinking about that night and how I had swum

beneath the surface of the river when I heard footsteps approaching along the bank: The ground was soft and damp and the footfall was muffled, but whoever it was was quite close. I should have left then but I was curious to see who would come to the river at this time of night, and I knew he would not see me.

He was a man of less than average height and very slight; in the darkness I could make out nothing else. He looked around furtively and then knelt at the water's edge as if he were praying. The wind blew off the river, bringing the tang of water and mud, and along with it the man's own smell.

His scent was somehow familiar. I sniffed the air like a dog, trying to place it. After a moment or two it came to me: It was the smell of the tannery. This man must be a leather worker, therefore an outcast. I knew then who he was: the man who had spoken to me after I had climbed into the castle. His brother had been one of the tortured Hidden to whom I had brought the release of death. I had used my second self on the riverbank, and this man had thought he had seen an angel and had spread the rumor of the Angel of Yamagata. I could guess why he was there praying. He must also be from the Hidden, maybe hoping to see the angel again. I remembered how the first time I saw him I had thought I had to kill him, but I had not been able to bring myself to do so. I gazed on him now with the troubled affection you have for someone whose life you have spared.

I felt something else, too; a pang of loss and regret for the certainties of my childhood, for the words and rituals that had comforted me then, seeming as eternal as the turn of the seasons and the passage of the moon and the stars in the sky. I had been plucked from my life among the Hidden when Shigeru had saved me at Mino. Since then I had kept my origins concealed, never speaking of them to anyone, never praying openly. But sometimes at night I still prayed after the manner of the faith I was raised in, to the Secret God that my mother worshipped, and now I felt a yearning to approach this man and talk to him.

As an Otori lord, even as a member of the Tribe, I should have shunned a leather worker, for they slaughter animals and are considered unclean, but the Hidden believe all men are created equal by the Secret God, and so I had been taught by my mother. Still, some vestige of caution kept me out of sight beneath the willow, though as I heard his whispered prayer I found my tongue repeating the words along with him.

I would have left it like that—I was not a complete fool, even though that night I was behaving like one—if I had not caught the sound of men approaching over the nearest bridge. It was a patrol of some sort, probably Arai's men, though I had no way of knowing for sure. They must have stopped on the bridge and gazed down the river.

"There's that lunatic," I heard one say. "Makes me sick having to see him there night after night." His accent was local, but the next man who spoke sounded as if he came from the West.

"Give him a beating, he'll soon give up coming."

"We've done that. Makes no difference."

"Comes back for more, does he?"

"Let's lock him up for a few nights."

"Let's just chuck him in the river."

They laughed. I heard their footsteps grow louder as they began to run, and then fade a little as they passed behind a row of houses. They were still some way off; the man on the bank had heard nothing. I was not going to stand by and watch while the guards threw my man into the river. My man: He already belonged to me.

I slipped out from beneath the branches of the willow

and ran toward him. I tapped him on the shoulder and, when he turned, I hissed at him, "Come, hide quickly!"

He recognized me at once and, with a great gasp of amazement, threw himself at my feet, praying incoherently. In the distance I could hear the patrol approaching down the street that ran along the river. I shook the man, lifted his head, put my finger to my lips, and, trying to remember not to look him in the eye, pulled him into the shelter of the willows.

I should leave him here, I thought. *I can go invisible and avoid the patrol.* But then I heard them tramping round the corner and realized I was too late.

The breeze ruffled the water and set the willow leaves quivering. In the distance a cock crowed, a temple bell sounded.

"Gone!" a voice exclaimed, not ten paces from us.

Another man swore, "Filthy outcasts."

"Which is worse, do you reckon, outcasts or Hidden?"

"Some are both! That's the worst."

I heard the slicing sigh of a sword being drawn. One of the soldiers slashed at a clump of reeds and then at the willow itself. The man next to me tensed. He was trembling but he made no sound. The smell of tanned leather was so strong in my nostrils, I was sure the guards would catch it, but the rank smell of the river must have masked it.

I was thinking I might attract their attention away from the outcast—split my self and somehow evade them—when a pair of ducks, sleeping in the reeds, suddenly flew off, quacking loudly, skimming the surface of the water and shattering the quiet of the night. The men shouted in surprise, then jeered at each other. They joked and grumbled for a little longer, threw stones at the ducks, then left in the direction opposite the one they'd come from. I heard their footsteps echo through the town, fading until even I could hear them no more. I began to scold the man.

"What are you doing out at this time of night? They'd have thrown you in the river if they'd found you."

He bent his head to my feet again.

"Sit up," I urged him. "Speak to me."

He sat, glanced briefly upward at my face, and then dropped his eyes. "I come every night I can," he muttered. "I've been praying to God for one more sight of you. I can never forget what you did for my brother—for the rest of them." He was silent for a moment, then whispered, "I thought you were an angel. But people say you are Lord Otori's son. You killed Lord Iida in revenge for his death. Now we have a new lord, Arai Daiichi from Kumamoto. His men have been combing the town for you. I thought they must know you were here. So I came tonight again to see you. Whatever form you choose to come in, you must be one of God's angels to do what you did."

It was a shock to hear my story repeated by this man. It brought home to me the danger I was in. "Go home. Tell no one you saw me." I prepared to leave.

He did not seem to hear me. He was in an almost exalted state: his eyes glittering, flecks of spittle shimmering on his lips. "Stay, lord," he exhorted me. "Every night I bring food for you, food and wine. We must share them together; then you must bless me and I will die happy."

He took up a small bundle. Unwrapping the food and placing it on the ground between us, he began to say the first prayer of the Hidden. The familiar words made my neck tingle, and when he'd finished I responded quietly with the second prayer. Together we made the sign over the food and over ourselves, and I began to eat.

The meal was pitifully sparse, a millet cake with a trace

of smoked fish skin buried in it, but it had all the elements of the rituals of my childhood. The outcast brought out a small flask and poured from it into a wooden bowl. It was some home-brewed liquor, far rougher than wine, and we had no more than a mouthful each, but the smell reminded me of my home. I felt my mother's presence strongly and tears pricked my eyelids.

"Are you a priest?" I whispered, wondering how he had escaped the Tohan persecution.

"My brother was our priest. The one you released in mercy. Since his death I do what I can for our people—those who are left."

"Did many die under Iida?"

"In the East, hundreds. My parents fled here many years ago, and under the Otori there was no persecution. But in the ten years since Yaegahara, no one has been safe here. Now we have a new overlord, Arai: No one knows which way he will jump. They say he has other fish to gut. We may be left alone while he deals with the Tribe." His voice dropped to a whisper at this last word, as though just to utter it was to invite retribution. "And that would only be justice," he went on, "for it's they who are the murderers and the assassins.

Our people are harmless. We are forbidden to kill." He shot me an apologetic look. "Of course, lord, your case was different."

He had no idea how different, or how far I had gone from my mother's teaching. Dogs were barking in the distance, roosters announced the coming day. I had to go, yet I was reluctant to leave.

"You're not afraid?" I asked him.

"Often I am terrified. I don't have the gift of courage. But my life is in God's hands. He has some plan for me. He sent you to us."

"I am not an angel," I said.

"How else would one of the Otori know our prayers?" he replied. "Who but an angel would share food with someone like me?"

I knew the risk I was taking but I told him anyway. "Lord Shigeru rescued me from Iida at Mino."

I did not have to spell it out. He was silent for a moment, as if awed. Then he whispered, "Mino? We thought no one survived from there. How strange are the ways of God. You have been spared for some great purpose. If you are not an angel, you are marked by the Secret One."

I shook my head. "I am the least of beings. My life is not my own. Fate, which led me away from my own people, has now led me away from the Otori." I did not want to tell him I had become one of the Tribe.

"You need help?" he said. "We will always help you. Come to us at the outcasts' bridge."

"Where is that?"

"Where we tan the hides, between Yamagata and Tsuwano. Ask for Jo-An." He then said the third prayer, giving thanks for the food.

"I must go," I said.

"First would you give me a blessing, lord?"

I placed my right hand on his head and began the prayer my mother used to say to me. I felt uncomfortable, knowing I had little right to speak these words, but they came easily off my tongue. Jo-An took my hand and touched his forehead and lips to my fingers. I realized then how deeply he trusted me. He released my hand and bowed his head to the ground. When he raised it again, I was on the far side of the street. The sky was paling, the dawn air cool.

I slipped back from doorway to doorway. The temple bell rang out. The town was stirring, the first of the shutters were being taken down, and the smell of smoke from kitchen fires wafted through the streets. I had stayed far too long with Jo-An. I had not used my second self all night, but I felt split in half, as if I had left my true self permanently beneath the willow tree with him. The self that was returning to the Tribe was hollow.

When I came to the Muto house the nagging thought that had been at the back of my mind all night surfaced. How was I going to get across the overhang of the wall from the street? The white plaster, the gray tiles, shone in the dawn light, mocking me. I crouched in the shelter of the house opposite, deeply regretting my own rashness and stupidity. I'd lost my focus and concentration; my hearing was as acute as ever, but the inner certainty, the instinct, was gone.

I couldn't stay where I was. In the distance I heard the tramp of feet, the padding of hoofs. A group of men was approaching. Their voices floated toward me. I thought I recognized the Western accent that would mark them as Arai's men. I knew that if they found me, my life with the Tribe would be over: My life would probably be over altogether if Arai was as insulted as had been said.

I had no choice but to run to the gate and shout to the

guards to open it, but as I was about to cross the street, I heard voices from beyond the wall. Akio was calling quietly to the guards. There was a creak and a thud as the gate was unbarred.

The patrol turned into the far end of the street. I went invisible, ran to the gate, and slipped inside.

The guards did not see me but Akio did, just as he had forestalled me at Inuyama when the Tribe first seized me. He stepped into my path and grabbed both arms.

I braced myself for the blows I was certain would follow, but he did not waste any time. He pulled me swiftly toward the house.

The horses of the patrol were moving faster now, coming down the street at a trot. I stumbled over the dog. It whimpered in its sleep. The riders shouted to the guards at the gate, "Good morning!"

"What've you got there?" one of the guards replied.

"None of your business!"

As Akio pulled me up into the house I looked back. Through the narrow space between the bathhouse and the wall, I could just see the open gate and the street beyond.

Behind the horses two men on foot were dragging a captive

between them. I could not see him clearly but I could hear his voice. I could hear his prayers. It was my outcast, Jo-An.

I must have made a lunge off the step toward the gate, for Akio pulled me back with a force that almost dislocated my shoulder. Then he did hit me, silently and efficiently on the side of the neck. The room spun sickeningly. Still without speaking, he dragged me into the main room, where the maid was sweeping the matting. She took no notice of us at all.

He called out to the kitchen as he opened the wall of the hidden room and pushed me inside. Kenji's wife came into the room and Akio slid the door shut.

Her face was pale and her eyes puffy, as though she were still fighting sleep. I could feel her fury before she spoke. She slapped me twice across the face. "You little bastard! You half-bred idiot! How dare you do that to me."

Akio pushed me to the floor, still holding my arms behind my back. I lowered my head in submission. There didn't seem to be any point in saying anything.

"Kenji warned me you'd try to get out. I didn't believe him. Why did you do it?"

When I didn't reply, she knelt, too, and raised my head so she could see my face. I kept my eyes turned away.

"Answer me! Are you insane?"

"Just to see if I could."

She sighed in exasperation, sounding like her husband.

"I don't like being shut in," I muttered.

"It's madness," Akio said angrily. "He's a danger to us all. We should—"

She interrupted him swiftly. "That decision can only be taken by the Kikuta master. Until then, our task is to try to keep him alive and out of Arai's hands." She gave me another cuff round the head, but a less serious one. "Who saw you?"

"No one. Just an outcast."

"What outcast?"

"A leather worker. Jo-An."

"Jo-An? The lunatic? The one who saw the angel?" She took a deep breath. "Don't tell me he saw you."

"We talked for a while," I admitted.

"Arai's men have already picked the outcast up," Akio said.

"I hope you realize just what a fool you are," she said.

I bowed my head again. I was thinking about Jo-An, wishing I'd seen him home—if he had any home in Yamagata—wondering if I could rescue him, demanding silently to know what his god's purpose was for him now. *I am often afraid,* he had said. *Terrified.* Pity and remorse twisted my heart.

"Find out what the outcast gives away," Kenji's wife said to Akio.

"He won't betray me," I said.

"Under torture, everyone betrays," he replied briefly.

"We should hasten your journey," she went on. "Perhaps you should even leave today."

Akio was still kneeling behind me, holding me by the wrists. I felt the movement as he nodded.

"Is he to be punished?" he said.

"No, he has to be able to travel. Besides, as you should have realized by now, physical punishment makes no impression on him. However, make sure he knows exactly what the outcast suffers. His head may be stubborn but his heart is soft."

"The masters say it is his main weakness," Akio remarked.

"Yes, if it weren't for that we might have another Shintaro."

"Soft hearts can be hardened," Akio muttered.

"Well, you Kikuta know best how to do that."

I remained kneeling on the floor while they discussed me as coldly as if I were some commodity, a vat of wine, perhaps, that might turn out to be a particularly fine one or might be tainted and worthless.

"What now?" Akio said. "Is he to be tied up until we leave?"

"Kenji said you chose to come to us," she said to me. "If that's true, why do you try to escape?"

"I came back."

"Will you try again?"

"No."

"You will go to Matsue with the actors and do nothing to endanger them or yourself?"

"Yes."

She thought for a moment and told Akio to tie me up anyway. After he'd done so, they left me to make the preparations for our departure. The maid came with a tray of food and tea and helped me to eat and drink without saying a word. After she had taken away the bowls, no one came near me. I listened to the sound of the house and thought I discerned all the harshness and cruelty that lay beneath its everyday song. A huge weariness came over me. I crawled to the mattress, made myself as comfortable as I could, thought hopelessly of Jo-An and my own stupidity, and fell asleep.

I woke suddenly, my heart pounding, my throat dry. I had been dreaming of the outcast, a terrible dream in which, from far away, an insistent voice, as small as a mosquito's, was whispering something only I could hear.

Akio must have had his face pressed up against the outside wall. He described every detail of Jo-An's torture at the hands of Arai's men. It went on and on in a slow monotone, making my skin crawl and my stomach turn. Now and then he would fall silent for long periods; I would think with relief it was over, then his voice would begin again.

I could not even put my fingers in my ears. There was no escape from it. Kenji's wife was right: It was the worst punishment she could have devised for me. I wished above all I had killed the outcast when I first saw him on the riverbank. Pity had stayed my hand then, but that pity had had fatal results. I would have given Jo-An a swift and merciful death. Now, because of me, he was suffering torment.

When Akio's voice finally died away, I heard Yuki's tread outside. She stepped into the room carrying a bowl, scissors, and a razor. The maid, Sadako, followed her with an armful of clothes, placed them on the floor, and then went silently out of the room. I heard Sadako tell Akio that the midday meal was ready and heard him get to his feet and follow her to the kitchen. The smell of food floated through the house, but I had no appetite.

"I have to cut your hair," Yuki said. I still wore it in the warrior style, restrained as Ichiro, my former teacher in Shigeru's household, had insisted, but unmistakable, the forehead shaved, the back hair caught up in a topknot. It had not been trimmed for weeks, nor had I shaved my face, though I still had very little beard.

Yuki untied my hands and legs and made me sit in front of her. "You are an idiot," she said as she began to cut.

I didn't answer. I was already aware of that but also knew I would probably do the same thing again.

"My mother was so angry. I don't know which surprised her more: that you were able to put her to sleep, or that you dared to."

Bits of hair were falling around me. "At the same time

she was almost excited," Yuki went on. "She says you remind her of Shintaro when he was your age."

"She knew him?"

"I'll tell you a secret: She burned for him. She'd have married him, but it didn't suit the Tribe, so she married my father instead. Anyway, I don't think she could bear for anyone to have that power over her. Shintaro was a master of the Kikuta sleep: No one was safe from him."

Yuki was animated, more chatty than I'd ever known her. I could feel her hand trembling slightly against my neck as the scissors snipped cold on my scalp. I remembered Kenji's dismissive words about his wife, the girls he'd slept with. Their marriage was like most, an arranged alliance between two families.

"If she'd married Shintaro, I would have been someone else," Yuki said pensively. "I don't think she ever stopped loving him, in her heart."

"Even though he was a murderer?"

"He wasn't a murderer! No more than you are."

Something in her voice told me the conversation was moving onto dangerous ground. I found Yuki very attractive. I knew she had strong feelings for me. But I did not feel for her what I had felt for Kaede, and I did not want to be talking about love.

I tried to change the subject. "I thought the sleep thing was something only Kikuta do. Wasn't Shintaro from the Kuroda family?"

"On his father's side. His mother was Kikuta. Shintaro and your father were cousins."

It chilled me to think that the man whose death I'd caused, whom everyone said I resembled, should have been a relative.

"What exactly happened the night Shintaro died?" Yuki said curiously.

"I heard someone climbing into the house. The window of the first floor was open because of the heat. Lord Shigeru wanted to take him alive, but when he seized him, we all three fell into the garden. The intruder struck his head on a rock, but we thought he also took poison in the moment of the fall. Anyway, he died without regaining consciousness. Your father confirmed it was Kuroda Shintaro. Later we learned that Shigeru's uncles, the Otori lords, had hired him to assassinate Shigeru."

"It's extraordinary," Yuki said, "that you should have been there and no one knew who you were."

I answered her unguardedly, disarmed, perhaps, by the memories of that night. "Not so extraordinary. Shigeru was looking for me when he rescued me at Mino. He already knew of my existence and knew my father had been an assassin." Lord Shigeru had told me this when we had talked in Tsuwano. I had asked him if that was why he had sought me out, and he had told me it was the main reason but not the only one. I never found out what the other reasons might have been, and now I never would.

Yuki's hands had gone still. "My father was not aware of that."

"No, he was allowed to believe that Shigeru acted on an impulse, that he saved my life and brought me back to Hagi purely by chance."

"You can't be serious?"

Too late, her intensity aroused my suspicions. "What does it matter now?"

"How did Lord Otori find out something that even the Tribe had not suspected? What else did he tell you?"

"He told me many things," I said impatiently. "He and Ichiro taught me almost everything I know."

"I mean about the Tribe!"

I shook my head as if I did not understand. "Nothing. I know nothing about the Tribe other than what your father taught me and what I've learned here."

She stared at me. I avoided looking at her directly. "There's a whole lot more to learn," she said finally. "I'll be able to teach you on the road." She ran her hands over my cropped hair and stood in one movement, as her mother had. "Put these on. I'll bring you something to eat."

"I'm not hungry," I said, reaching over and picking up the clothes. Once brightly colored, they had faded to dull orange and brown. I wondered who had worn them and what had befallen him on the road.

"We have many hours of travel ahead," she said. "We may not eat again today. Whatever Akio and I tell you to do, you do. If we tell you to brew the dirt under our fingernails and drink it, you do it. If we say eat, you eat. And you don't do anything else. We learned this sort of obedience when we were children. You have to learn it now."

I wanted to ask her if she had been obedient when she'd brought Shigeru's sword, Jato, to me in Inuyama, but it seemed wiser to say nothing. I changed into the actor's clothes, and when Yuki came back with food, I ate without question.

She watched me silently, and when I finished she said, "The outcast is dead."

They wanted my heart hardened. I did not look at her or reply.

"He said nothing about you," she went on. "I did not know an outcast would have such courage. He had no poison to release himself. Yet, he said nothing."

I thanked Jo-An in my heart, thanked the Hidden who take their secrets with them . . . where? Into Paradise? Into another life? Into the silencing fire, the silent grave? I wanted to pray for him, after the fashion of our people. Or light candles and burn incense for him, as Ichiro and Chiyo had taught me in Shigeru's house in Hagi. I thought of Jo-An going alone into the dark. What would his people do without him?

"Do you pray to anyone?" I asked Yuki.

"Of course," she said, surprised.

"Who to?"

"The Enlightened One, in all his forms. The gods of the mountain, the forest, the river: all the old ones. This morning I took rice and flowers to the shrine at the bridge to ask a blessing on our journey. I'm glad we're leaving today after all.

It's a good day for traveling: All the signs are favorable." She looked at me as if she were thinking it all over, then shook her head. "Don't ask things like that. It makes you sound so different. No one else would ask that."

"No one else has lived my life."

"You're one of the Tribe now. Try and behave like it."

She took a small bag from inside her sleeve and passed it to me. "Here. Akio said to give you these."

I opened it and felt inside, then tipped the contents out. Five juggler's balls, smooth and firm, packed with rice grain, fell to the floor. Much as I hated juggling, it was impossible not to pick them up and handle them. With three in my right hand and two in my left, I stood up. The feel of the balls, the actor's clothes, had already turned me into someone else.

"You are Minoru," Yuki said. "These would have been given to you by your father. Akio is your older brother; I'm your sister."

"We don't look very alike," I said, tossing the balls up.

"We will become alike enough," Yuki replied. "My father said you could change your features to some extent."

"What happened to our father?" Round and back the balls went, the circle, the fountain . . .

"He's dead."

"Convenient."

She ignored me. "We're traveling to Matsue for the autumn festival. It will take five or six days, depending on the weather. Arai still has men looking for you, but the main search here is over. He has already left for Inuyama. We travel in the opposite direction. At night we have safe houses to go to. But the road belongs to no one. If we meet any patrols, you'll have to prove who you are."

I dropped one of the balls and bent to retrieve it.

"You can't drop them," Yuki said. "No one of your age ever drops them. My father also said you could impersonate well. Don't bring any of us into danger."

We left from the back entrance. Kenji's wife came out to bid us farewell. She looked me over, checked my hair and clothes. "I hope we meet again," she said. "But, knowing your recklessness, I hardly expect it."

I bowed to her, saying nothing. Akio was already in the yard with a handcart like the one I'd been bundled into in Inuyama. He told me to get inside and I climbed in among the props and costumes. Yuki handed me my knife. I was pleased to see it again and tucked it away inside my clothes.

Akio lifted the cart handles and began to push. I rocked through the town in semidarkness, listening to its sounds and to the speech of the actors. I recognized the voice of the other girl from Inuyama, Keiko. There was one other man with us, too; I'd heard his voice in the house but had not set eyes on him.

When we were well beyond the last houses, Akio stopped, opened the side of the cart, and told me to get out. It was about the second half of the Hour of the Goat and still very warm, despite the onset of autumn. Akio gleamed with sweat. He had removed most of his clothes to push the cart. I could see how strong he was. He was taller than me, and much more muscular. He went to drink from the stream that ran beside the road and splashed water onto his head and face. Yuki, Keiko, and the older man were squatting by the side of the road. I would hardly have recognized any of them. They were completely transformed into a troupe of actors making a precarious living from town to town, existing on their wits and talents, always on the verge of starvation or crime.

The man gave me a grin, showing his missing teeth. His face was lean, expressive, and slightly sinister. Keiko ignored me. Like Akio, she had half-healed scars on one hand, from my knife.

I took a deep breath. Hot as it was, it was infinitely better than the room I'd been shut up in and the stifling cart. Behind us lay the town of Yamagata, the castle white against the mountains, which were still mostly green and luxuriant, with splashes of color here and there where the leaves had started to turn. The rice fields were turning gold, too. It would soon be harvesttime. To the southwest I could see the steep slope of Terayama, but the roofs of the temple were invisible behind the cedars. Beyond lay fold after fold of mountains, turning blue in the distance, shimmering in the afternoon haze. Silently I said farewell to Shigeru, reluctant to turn away and break my last tie with him and with my life as one of the Otori.

Akio gave me a blow on the shoulder. "Stop dreaming like an imbecile," he said, his voice changed into a rougher accent and dialect. "It's your turn to push."

By the time evening came I'd conceived the deepest hatred possible for that cart. It was heavy and unwieldy, blistering the hands and straining the back. Pulling it uphill was bad enough, as the wheels caught in potholes and ruts and it took all of us to get it free, but hanging on to it downhill was even harder. I would happily have let go and sent it hurtling into the forest. I thought longingly of my horse, Raku.

The older man, Kazuo, walked alongside me, helping me to adjust my accent and telling me the words I needed to know in the private language of actors. Some Kenji had already taught me, the dark street slang of the Tribe; some were new to me. I mimicked him, as I'd mimicked Ichiro, my Otori teacher, in a very different kind of learning, and tried to think myself into becoming Minoru.

Toward the end of the day, when the light was beginning to fade, we descended a slope toward a village. The road leveled out and the surface grew smoother. A man walking home called the evening greeting to us.

I could smell wood smoke and food cooking. All around me rose the sounds of the village at the end of the day: the splash of water as the farmers washed, children playing and squabbling, women gossiping as they cooked, the crackle of the fires, the chink of ax on wood, the shrine bell, the whole web of life that I'd been raised in.

And I caught something else: the clink of a bridle, the muffled stamp of a horse's feet.

"There's a patrol ahead," I said to Kazuo.

He held up his hand for us to stop and called quietly to Akio, "Minoru says there's a patrol."

Akio squinted at me against the setting sun. "You heard them?"

"I can hear horses. What else would it be?"

He nodded and shrugged as if to say, *As good now as anytime.* "Take the cart."

As I took Akio's place Kazuo began to sing a rowdy comic song. He had a good voice. It rang out into the still evening air. Yuki reached into the cart and took out a small drum, which she threw to Akio. Catching it, he began to beat out the rhythm of the song. Yuki also brought out a one-stringed instrument that she twanged as she walked beside us. Keiko had spinning tops, like the ones that had captured my attention at Inuyama.

Singing and playing, we rounded the corner and came to the patrol. They had set up a bamboo barrier just before the first houses of the village. There were about nine or ten men, most of them sitting on the ground, eating. They wore Arai's bear crest on their jackets; the setting-sun banners of the Seishuu had been erected on the bank. Four horses grazed beneath them.

A swarm of children hung around, and when they saw us they ran toward us, shouting and giggling. Kazuo broke off his song to direct a couple of riddles at them and then shouted impudently to the soldiers, "What's going on, lads?"

Their commander rose to his feet and approached us. We all immediately dropped to the dust.

"Get up," he said. "Where've you come from?" He had a squarish face with heavy brows, a thin mouth, and a clenched jaw. He wiped the rice from his lips on the back of his hand.

"Yamagata." Akio handed the drum to Yuki and held out a wooden tablet. It had our names inscribed on it, the name of our guild and our license from the city. The commander gazed at it for a long time, deciphering our names, every now and then looking across at each of us in turn, scanning our faces. Keiko was spinning the tops. The men watched her with more than idle interest. Players were the same as prostitutes as far as they were concerned. One of them made a mocking suggestion to her; she laughed back.

I leaned against the cart and wiped the sweat from my face.

"What's he do, Minoru?" the commander said, handing the tablet back to Akio.

"My younger brother? He's a juggler. It's the family calling."

"Let's see him," the commander said, his thin lips parting in a sort of smile.

Akio did not hesitate for a moment. "Hey, Little Brother. Show the lord."

I wiped my hands on my headband and tied it back round my head. I took the balls from the bag, felt their smooth weight, and in an instant became Minoru. This was my life. I had never known any other: the road, the new village, the suspicious, hostile stares. I forgot my tiredness, my aching head and blistered hands. I was Minoru, doing what I'd done since I was old enough to stand.

The balls flew in the air. I did four first, then five. I'd just finished the second sequence of the fountain when Akio jerked his head at me. I let the balls flow in his direction. He caught them effortlessly, throwing the tablet into the air with them. Then he sent them back to me. The sharp edge of the tablet caught my blistered palm. I was angry with him, wondering what his intention was: to show me up? To betray me?

I lost the rhythm. Tablet and balls fell into the dust.

The smile left the commander's face. He took a step forward. In that moment a mad impulse came into my mind: to give myself up to him, throw myself on Arai's mercy, escape the Tribe before it was too late.

Akio seemed to fly toward me. "Idiot!" he yelled, giving me a cuff round the ear. "Our father would cry out from his grave!"

As soon as he raised his hand to me, I knew my disguise would not be penetrated. It would have been unthinkable for an actor to strike an Otori warrior. The blow turned me into Minoru again, as nothing else could have done.

"Forgive me, Older Brother," I said, picking up the balls and the tablet; I kept them spinning in the air until the commander laughed and waved us forward.

"Come and see us tonight!" Keiko called to the soldiers.

"Yes, tonight," they called back.

Kazuo began to sing again, Yuki to beat the drum. I threw the tablet to Akio and put the balls away. They were darkened with blood. I picked up the handles of the cart. The barrier was lifted aside and we walked through to the village beyond.

· 4 ·

Kaede set out on the last day of her journey home on a perfect autumn morning, the sky clear blue, the air cool and thin as springwater. Mist hung in the valleys and above the river, silvering spiders' webs and the tendrils of wild clematis. But just before noon the weather began to change. Clouds crept over the sky from the northwest, and the wind swung. The light seemed to fade early, and before evening it began to rain.

The rice fields, vegetable gardens, and fruit trees had all been severely damaged by storms. The villages seemed half-empty, and the few people around stared sullenly at her, bowing only when threatened by the guards and then with bad grace. She did not know if they recognized her or not; she did not want to linger among them, but she could not help wondering why the damage was unrepaired, why the men were not working in the fields to salvage what they could of the harvest.

Her heart did not know how to behave. Sometimes it slowed in foreboding, making her feel that she might faint, and then it sped up, beating frantically in excitement and fear. The miles left to travel seemed endless, and yet, the horses' steady step ate them up all too quickly. She was afraid above all of what faced her at home.

She kept seeing views she thought were familiar, and her heart would leap in her throat, but when they came at last to the walled garden and the gates of her parents' home, she did not recognize any of it. Surely this was not where she lived? It was so small; it was not even fortified and guarded. The gates stood wide open. As Raku stepped through them Kaede could not help gasping.

Shizuka had already slid from the horse's back. She looked up. "What is it, lady?"

"The garden!" Kaede exclaimed. "What happened to it?"

Everywhere were signs of the ferocity of the storms. An uprooted pine tree lay across the stream. In its fall it had knocked over and crushed a stone lantern. Kaede had a flash of memory: the lantern, newly erected, a light burning in it, evening, the Festival of the Dead perhaps; a lamp floated away downstream, and she felt her mother's hand against her hair.

She gazed, uncomprehending, at the ruined garden. It was more than storm damage. Obviously it had been months since anyone had tended the shrubs or the moss, cleared out the pools, or pruned the trees. Was this her house, one of the key domains of the West? What had happened to the once powerful Shirakawa?

The horse lowered his head and rubbed it against his foreleg. He whinnied, impatient and tired, expecting now that they had stopped to be unsaddled and fed.

"Where are the guards?" Kaede said. "Where is everyone?"

The man she called Scar, the captain of the escort, rode his horse up to the veranda, leaned forward, and shouted, "Hello! Anyone within?"

"Don't go in," she called to him. "Wait for me. I will go inside first."

Long Arm was standing by Raku's head, holding the bridle. Kaede slid from the horse's back into Shizuka's arms. The rain had turned to a fine, light drizzle that beaded their hair and clothes. The garden smelled rankly of dampness and decay, sour earth, and fallen leaves. Kaede felt the image of her childhood home, kept intact and glowing in her heart for eight long years, intensify unbearably, and then it vanished forever.

Long Arm gave the bridle to one of the foot soldiers and, drawing his sword, went in front of Kaede. Shizuka followed them.

As she stepped out of her sandals onto the veranda, it seemed the feel of the wood was faintly familiar to her feet. But she did not recognize the smell of the house at all. It was a stranger's home.

There was a sudden movement from within, and Long Arm leaped forward into the shadows. A girl's voice cried out in alarm. The man pulled her onto the veranda.

"Let go of her," Kaede commanded in fury. "How dare you touch her?"

"He is only protecting you," Shizuka murmured, but Kaede was not listening. She stepped toward the girl, taking her hands and staring into her face. She was almost the same height as Kaede, with a gentle face and light-brown eyes like their father's.

"Ai? I am your sister, Kaede. Don't you remember me?"

The girl gazed back. Her eyes filled with tears. "Sister? Is it really you? For a moment, against the light . . . I thought you were our mother."

Kaede took her sister in her arms, feeling tears spring into her own eyes. "She's dead, isn't she?"

"Over two months ago. Her last words were of you. She longed to see you, but the knowledge of your marriage brought her peace." Ai's voice faltered and she drew back from Kaede's embrace. "Why have you come here? Where is your husband?"

"Have you had no news from Inuyama?"

"We have been battered by typhoons this year. Many people died and the harvest was ruined. We've heard so little—only rumors of war. After the last storm an army swept through, but we hardly understood who they were fighting for or why."

"Arai's army?"

"They were Seishuu from Maruyama and farther south. They were going to join Lord Arai against the Tohan. Father was outraged, for he considered himself an ally to Lord Iida. He tried to stop them from passing through here. He met them near the Sacred Caves. They attempted to reason with him, but he attacked them."

"Father fought them? Is he dead?"

"No, he was defeated, of course, and most of his men were killed, but he still lives. He thinks Arai a traitor and an upstart. He had sworn allegiance, after all, to the Noguchi when you went as a hostage."

"The Noguchi were overthrown, I am no longer a hostage, and I am in alliance with Arai," Kaede said.

Her sister's eyes widened. "I don't understand. I don't understand any of it." She seemed conscious for the first time of Shizuka and the men outside. She made a helpless gesture. "Forgive me, you must be exhausted. You have come a long way. The men must be hungry." She frowned, suddenly looking like a child. "What shall I do?" she whispered. "We have so little to offer you."

"Are there no servants left?"

"I sent them to hide in the forest when we heard the horses. I think they will come back before nightfall."

"Shizuka," Kaede said, "go to the kitchen and see what there is. Prepare food and drink for the men. They may rest here tonight. I shall need at least ten to stay on with me." She pointed at Long Arm. "Let him pick them. The others must return to Inuyama. If they harm any of my people or my possessions in any way, they will answer with their lives."

Shizuka bowed. "Lady."

"I'll show you the way," Ai said, and led Shizuka toward the back of the house.

"What is your name?" Kaede said to Long Arm.

He dropped to his knees before her. "Kondo, lady."

"Are you one of Lord Arai's men?"

"My mother was from the Seishuu. My father, if I may trust you with my secrets, was from the Tribe. I fought with Arai's men at Kushimoto, and was asked to enter his service."

She looked down at him. He was not a young man. His hair was gray-streaked, the skin on his neck lined. She wondered what his past had been, what work he had done for the Tribe, how far she could trust him. But she needed a man to handle the soldiers and the horses and defend the house; Kondo had saved Shizuka, he was feared and respected by Arai's other men, and he had the fighting skills she required.

"I may need your help for a few weeks," she said. "Can I depend on you?"

He looked up at her then. In the gathering darkness she could not make out his expression. His teeth gleamed white as he smiled, and when he spoke his voice had a ring of sincerity, even devotion. "Lady Otori can depend on me as long as she needs me."

"Swear it, then," she said, feeling herself flush as she pretended an authority she was not sure she possessed.

The lines around his eyes crinkled momentarily. He touched his forehead to the matting and swore allegiance to her and her family, but she thought she detected a note of irony in his voice. *The Tribe always dissemble,* she thought, chilled. *Moreover, they answer only to themselves.*

"Go and select ten men you can trust," she said. "See how much feed there is for the horses, and if the barns provide shelter enough."

"Lady Otori," he replied, and again she thought she heard irony. She wondered how much he knew, how much Shizuka had told him.

After a few moments Ai returned, took Kaede's hand, and said quietly, "Should I tell Father?"

"Where is he? What is his condition? Was he wounded?"

"He was wounded slightly. But it is not the injury. . . . Our mother's death, the loss of so many men . . . sometimes his mind seems to wander, and he does not seem to know where he is. He talks to ghosts and apparitions."

"Why did he not take his own life?"

"When he was first brought back, he wanted to." Ai's voice broke completely and she began to weep. "I prevented him. I was so weak. Hana and I clung to him and begged him not to leave us. I took away his weapons." She turned her tear-streaked face to Kaede. "It's all my fault. I should have had more courage. I should have helped him to die and then killed myself and Hana, as a warrior's daughter should. But I couldn't do it. I couldn't take her life, and I couldn't leave her alone. So we live in shame, and it is driving Father mad."

Kaede thought, *I also should have killed myself, as soon as I heard Lord Shigeru had been betrayed. But I did not. Instead, I killed Iida.* She touched Ai on the cheek, felt the wetness of tears.

"Forgive me," Ai whispered. "I have been so weak."

"No," Kaede replied. "Why should you die?" Her sister was only thirteen; she had committed no crime. "Why should any of us choose death?" she said. "We will live instead. Where is Hana now?"

"I sent her to the forest with the women."

Kaede had rarely felt compassion before. Now it woke within her, as painful as grief. She remembered how the White Goddess had come to her. The All-Merciful One had consoled her, had promised that Takeo would return to her. But together with the goddess's promise had come the demands of compassion, that Kaede should live to take care of her sisters, her people, her unborn child. From outside she could hear Kondo's voice giving orders, the men shouting in reply. A horse whinnied and another answered. The rain had strengthened, beating out a pattern of sound that seemed familiar to her.

"I must see Father," she said. "Then we must feed the men. Will anyone help from the villages?"

"Just before Mother died, the farmers sent a delegation. They were complaining about the rice tax, the state of the dikes and fields, the loss of the harvest. Father was furious. He refused even to talk to them. Ayame persuaded them to leave us alone because Mother was sick. Since then everything has been in confusion. The villagers are afraid of Father: They say he is cursed."

"What about our neighbors?"

"There is Lord Fujiwara. He used to visit Father occasionally."

"I don't remember him. What sort of a man is he?"

"He's strange. Rather elegant and cold. He is of very

high birth, they say, and used to live in the capital."

"Inuyama?"

"No, the real capital, where the Emperor lives."

"He is a nobleman, then?"

"I suppose he must be. He speaks differently from people round here. I can hardly understand him. He seems a very erudite man. Father liked talking to him about history and the classics."

"Well, if he ever calls on Father again, perhaps I will seek his advice." Kaede was silent for a moment. She was fighting weariness. Her limbs ached and her belly felt heavy. She longed to lie down and sleep. And somewhere within herself she felt guilty that she was not grieving more. It was not that she did not suffer anguish for her mother's death and her father's humiliation, but she had no space left in her soul for any more grief, and no energy to give to it.

She looked round the room. Even in the twilight she could see the matting was old, the walls water-stained, the screens torn. Ai followed her gaze. "I'm ashamed," she whispered. "There's been so much to do, and so much I don't know how to do."

"I almost seem to remember how it used to be," Kaede said. "It had a glow about it."

"Mother made it like that," Ai said, stifling a sob.

"We will make it like that again," Kaede promised.

From the direction of the kitchen there suddenly came the sound of someone singing. Kaede recognized Shizuka's voice, and the song as the one she had heard the first time she met her, the love ballad about the village and the pine tree.

How does she have the courage to sing now? she thought, and then Shizuka came quickly into the room carrying a lamp in each hand.

"I found these in the kitchen," she said, "and luckily the fire was still burning. Rice and barley are cooking. Kondo has sent men to the village to buy whatever they can. And the household women have returned."

"Our sister will be with them," Ai said, breathing a sigh of relief.

"Yes, she has brought an armful of herbs and mushrooms that she insists on cooking."

Ai blushed. "She has become half-wild," she began to explain.

"Let me see her," Kaede said. "Then you must take me to Father."

Ai went out, Kaede heard a few words of argument from the kitchen, and seconds later Ai returned with a girl of about nine years old.

"This is our older sister, Kaede. She left home when you were a baby," Ai said to Hana, and then, prompting her, "greet your older sister properly."

"Welcome home," Hana whispered, then dropped to her knees and bowed to Kaede. Kaede knelt in front of her, took her hands, and raised her. She looked into her face.

"I was younger than you are now when I left home," she said, studying the fine eyes, the perfect bone structure beneath the childish roundness.

"She is like you, lady," Shizuka said.

"I hope she will be happier," Kaede replied, and, drawing Hana to her, hugged her. She felt the slight body begin to shake, and realized the child was crying.

"Mother! I want Mother!"

Kaede's own eyes filled with tears.

"Hush, Hana, don't cry, little sister." Ai tried to soothe

her. "I'm sorry," she said to Kaede. "She is still grieving. She has not been taught how to behave."

Well, she will learn, Kaede thought, *as I had to. She will learn not to let her feelings show, to accept that life is made up of suffering and loss, to cry in private if she cries at all.*

"Come," Shizuka said, taking Hana by the hand. "You have to show me how to cook the mushrooms. I don't know these local ones."

Her eyes met Kaede's above the child's head, and her smile was warm and cheerful.

"Your woman is wonderful," Ai said as they left. "How long has she been with you?"

"She came to me a few months ago, just before I left Noguchi Castle," Kaede replied. The two sisters remained kneeling on the floor, not knowing what to say to each other. The rain fell heavily now, streaming from the eaves like a curtain of steel arrows. It was nearly dark. Kaede thought, *I cannot tell Ai that Lord Arai himself sent Shizuka to me, as part of the conspiracy to overthrow Iida, or that Shizuka is from the Tribe. I cannot tell her anything. She is so young, she has never left Shirakawa, she knows nothing of the world.*

"I suppose we should go to Father," she said.

But at that moment she heard his voice calling from a distant part of the house. "Ai! Ayame!" His footsteps approached. He was complaining softly. "Ah, they've all gone away and left me. These worthless women!"

He came into the room and stopped short when he saw Kaede.

"Who's there? Do we have visitors? Who's come at this time of night in the rain?"

Ai stood and went to him. "It's Kaede, your oldest daughter. She has returned. She's safe."

"Kaede?" He took a step toward her. She did not stand but, remaining where she was, bowed deeply, touching her forehead to the floor.

Ai helped her father down. He knelt in front of Kaede. "Sit up, sit up," he said impatiently. "Let us see the worst in each other."

"Father?" she questioned as she raised her head.

"I am a shamed man," he said. "I should have died. I did not. I am hollow now, only partly alive. Look at me, daughter."

It was true that terrible changes had been wrought in him. He had always been controlled and dignified. Now he seemed a husk of his former self. There was a half-healed slash from temple to left ear; the hair had been shaved away from the wound. His feet were bare and his robe stained, his jaw was dark with stubble.

"What happened to you?" she said, trying to keep the anger out of her voice. She had come seeking refuge, looking for the lost childhood home she had spent eight years mourning, only to find it almost destroyed.

Her father made a weary gesture. "What does it matter? Everything is lost, ruined. Your return is the final blow. What happened to your marriage to Lord Otori? Don't tell me he is dead."

"Through no fault of mine," she said bitterly. "Iida murdered him."

His lips tightened and his face paled. "We have heard nothing here."

"Iida is also dead," she went on. "Arai's forces have taken Inuyama. The Tohan are overthrown."

The mention of Arai's name obviously disturbed him. "That traitor," he muttered, staring into the darkness as though ghosts gathered there. "He defeated Iida?" After a pause he went on, "I seem to have once again found myself on the losing side. My family must be under some curse. For the first time I am glad I have no son to inherit from me. Shirakawa can fade away, regretted by no one."

"You have three daughters!" Kaede responded, stung into anger.

"And my oldest is also cursed, bringing death to any man connected with her!"

"Iida caused Lord Otori's death! It was a plot from the start. My marriage was designed to bring him to Inuyama and into Iida's hands." The rain drummed hard against the roof, cascading from the eaves. Shizuka came in silently with more lamps, placed them on the floor, and knelt behind Kaede. *I must control myself,* Kaede thought. *I must not tell him everything.*

He was staring at her, his face puzzled. "So, are you married or not?"

Her heart was racing. She had never lied to her father. Now she found she could not speak. She turned her head away, as if overcome by grief.

Shizuka whispered. "May I speak, Lord Shirakawa?"

"Who is she?" he said to Kaede.

"She is my maid. She came to me at Noguchi Castle."

He nodded in Shizuka's direction. "What do you have to say?"

"Lady Shirakawa and Lord Otori were married secretly at Terayama," Shizuka said in a low voice. "Your kinswoman was witness, but she also died at Inuyama, along with her daughter."

"Maruyama Naomi is dead? Things get worse and worse. The domain will be lost to her stepdaughter's family now. We may as well hand over Shirakawa to them, too."

"I am her heir," Kaede said. "She entrusted everything to me."

He gave a short mirthless laugh. "They have disputed the domain for years. The husband is a cousin of Iida's, and is supported by many from both the Tohan and the Seishuu. You are mad if you think they will let you inherit."

Kaede felt rather than heard Shizuka stir slightly behind her. Her father was just the first man of many, an army, a whole clan—maybe even all the Three Countries—who would try to thwart her.

"All the same, I intend to."

"You'll have to fight for it," he said with scorn.

"Then I will fight." They sat for a few moments in silence

in the darkened room with the rain-drenched garden beyond.

"We have few men left," her father said, his voice bitter. "Will the Otori do anything for you? I suppose you must marry again. Have they suggested anyone?"

"It is too early to think of that," Kaede said. "I am still in mourning." She took a breath, so deep that she was sure he must hear it. "I believe I am carrying a child."

His eyes turned again to her, peering through the gloom. "Shigeru gave you a child?"

She bowed in confirmation, not daring to speak.

"Well, well," he said, suddenly inappropriately jovial. "We must celebrate! A man may have died but his seed lives. A remarkable achievement!" They had been talking in lowered voices, but now he shouted surprisingly loudly. "Ayame!"

Kaede jumped despite herself. She saw how his mind was loosened, swinging between lucidity and darkness. It frightened her, but she tried to put the fear aside. As long as he believed her for the time being, she would face whatever came afterward.

The woman Ayame came in and knelt before Kaede. "Lady, welcome home. Forgive us for such a sad homecoming."

Kaede stood, took her hands, and raised her to her feet.

They embraced. The solid indomitable figure that Kaede remembered had dwindled to a woman who was almost old. Yet, she thought she recalled her scent: It aroused sudden memories of childhood.

"Go and bring wine," Kaede's father commanded. "I want to drink to my grandchild."

Kaede felt a shiver of dread, as though by giving the child a false identity she had made its life false. "It is still so early," she said in a low voice. "Do not celebrate yet."

"Kaede!" Ayame exclaimed, using her name as she would to a child. "Don't say such things; don't tempt fate."

"Fetch wine," her father said loudly. "And close the shutters. Why do we sit here in the cold?"

As Ayame went toward the veranda they heard the sound of footsteps, and Kondo's voice called, "Lady Otori!"

Shizuka went to the doorway and spoke to him.

"Tell him to come up," Kaede said.

Kondo stepped onto the wooden floor and knelt in the entrance. Kaede was conscious of the swift glance he gave round the room, taking in in a moment the layout of the house, assessing the people in it. He spoke to her, not to her father.

"I've been able to get some food from the village. I've chosen the men you requested. A young man turned up, Amano Tenzo; he's taken charge of the horses. I'll see that the men get something to eat now, and set guards for the night."

"Thank you. We'll speak in the morning."

Kondo bowed again and left silently.

"Who's that fellow?" her father demanded. "Why did he not speak to me to ask my opinion or permission?"

"He works for me," Kaede replied.

"If he's one of Arai's men, I'll not have him in this house."

"I said, he works for me." Her patience was wearing thin. "We are in alliance with Lord Arai now. He controls most of the Three Countries. He is our overlord. You must accept this, Father. Iida is dead and everything has changed."

"Does that mean daughters may speak to their fathers so?"

"Ayame," Kaede said, "take my father to his room. He will eat there tonight."

Her father began to remonstrate. She raised her voice against him for the first time in her life. "Father, I am tired. We will talk tomorrow."

Ayame gave her a look that she chose to ignore. "Do as I

say," she said coldly, and after a moment the older woman obeyed and led her father away.

"You must eat, lady," Shizuka said. "Sit down; I'll bring you something."

"Make sure everyone is fed," Kaede said. "And close the shutters now."

Later she lay listening to the rain. Her household and her men were sheltered, fed after a fashion, safe, if Kondo could be trusted. She let the events of the day run through her mind, the problems she would have to deal with: her father, Hana, the neglected estate of Shirakawa, the disputed domain of Maruyama. How was she going to claim and keep what was hers?

If only I were a man, she thought. *How easy it would be. If I were Father's son, what would he not do for me?*

She knew she had the ruthlessness of a man. When she was still a hostage in Noguchi Castle, she had stabbed a guard without thinking, but Iida she had killed deliberately. She would kill again, rather than let any man crush her. Her thoughts drifted to Lady Maruyama. *I wish I had known you better,* she thought. *I wish I had been able to learn more from you. I am sorry for the pain I caused you. If only we had been able to talk freely.* She felt she saw the beautiful face before her, and heard her voice again. *I entrust my land and my people to you. Take care of them.*

I will, she promised. *I will learn how.* The meagerness of her education depressed her, but that could be remedied. She resolved she would find out how to run the estate, how to speak to the farmers, how to train men and fight battles—everything a son would have been taught from birth. *Father will have to teach me,* she thought. *It will give him something to think about apart from himself.*

She felt a twinge of emotion, fear or shame or, maybe, a combination of both. What was she turning into? Was she unnatural? Had she been bewitched or cursed? She was sure no woman had ever thought the way she did now. Except Lady Maruyama. Holding on to the lifeline of her promise to her kinswoman, she fell asleep at last.

The next morning she bade farewell to Arai's men, urging them to leave as soon as possible. They were happy to go, eager to return to the campaigns in the East before the onset of winter. Kaede was equally keen to get rid of them, fearing she could not afford to feed them for even one more night. Next she organized the household women to start cleaning the house and repairing the damage to the garden.

Shamefaced, Ayame confided in her that there was nothing to pay workmen with. Most of the Shirakawa treasures and all the money were gone.

"Then we must do what we can ourselves," Kaede said, and when the work was under way she went to the stables with Kondo.

A young man greeted her with a deference that could not hide his delight. It was Amano Tenzo, who had accompanied her father to Noguchi Castle, and whom she had known when they were both children. He was now about twenty years old.

"This is a fine horse," he said as he brought Raku forward and saddled him.

"He was a gift from Lord Otori's son," she said, stroking the horse's neck.

Amano beamed. "Otori horses are renowned for their stamina and good sense. They say they run them in the water meadows, and they're fathered by the river spirit. With your permission, we'll put our mares to him and get his foals next year."

She liked the way he addressed her directly and talked to her of such things. The stable area was in better condition than most of the grounds, clean and well maintained—though, apart from Raku, Amano's own chestnut stallion, and four horses belonging to Kondo and his men, there were only three other warhorses, all old and one lame. Horse skulls were fixed to the eaves, and the wind moaned through the empty eye sockets. She knew they were placed there to protect and calm the animals below, but at present the dead outnumbered the living.

"Yes, we must have more horses," she said. "How many mares do we have?"

"Only two or three at the moment."

"Can we get more before winter?"

He looked glum. "The war, the famine . . . this year has been disastrous for Shirakawa."

"You must show me the worst," she said. "Ride out with me now."

Raku's head was held high and his ears pricked forward. He seemed to be looking and listening. He whinnied softly at her approach but continued gazing into the distance.

"He misses someone—his master, I suppose," Amano said. "Don't let it worry you. He'll settle in with us and get over it."

She patted the horse's pale gray neck. *I miss him, too,* she whispered silently. *Will either of us ever get over it?* She felt the bond between herself and the little horse strengthen.

She rode out every morning, exploring her domain with Kondo and Amano. After a few days an older man turned up at the door and was greeted by the maids with tears of joy. It was Shoji Kiyoshi, her father's senior retainer, who had been wounded and feared dead. His knowledge of the estate, the villages, and the farmers was vast. Kaede swiftly realized he could tell her much of what she needed to know. At first he humored her, finding it strange and slightly comical that a girl should have such interests, but her quick grasp of affairs and her memory surprised him. He began to discuss problems with her, and though she never lost the feeling that he disapproved of her, she felt she could trust him.

Her father took little interest in the day-to-day management of the estate, and Kaede suspected he had been careless, even unjust, though it seemed disloyal to think it. He occupied the days with reading and writing in his rooms. She went to him every afternoon and sat watching him patiently. He spent a lot of time staring into the garden, saying nothing as Ayame and the maids worked tirelessly in it, but sometimes mumbling to himself, complaining about his fate.

She asked him to teach her, pleading, "Treat me as if I were your son," but he refused to take her seriously.

"A wife should be obedient and, if possible, beautiful. Men don't want women who think like them."

"They would always have someone to talk to," she argued.

"Men don't talk to their wives, they talk to each other," he retorted. "Anyway you have no husband. You would spend your time better marrying again."

"I will marry no one," she said. "That's why I must learn. All the things a husband would do for me, I must do for myself."

"Of course you will marry," he replied shortly. "Something will be arranged." But to her relief he made no efforts in that direction.

She continued to sit with him every day, kneeling beside him as he prepared the inkstone and the brushes, watching every stroke. She could read and write the flowing script that women used, but her father wrote in men's language, the shapes of the characters as impenetrable and solid as prison bars.

She watched patiently, until one day he handed her the brush and told her to write the characters for *man, woman,* and *child.*

Because she was naturally left-handed she took the brush in that hand, but, seeing him frown, transferred it to the right. Using her right hand meant, as always, that she had to put more effort into her work. She wrote boldly, copying his arm movements. He looked at the result for a long time.

"You write like a man," he said finally.

"Pretend that I am one." She felt his eyes on her and raised her own to meet his gaze. He was staring at her as if he did not know her, as if she alarmed and fascinated him at the same time, like some exotic animal.

"It would be interesting," he said, "to see if a girl could be taught. Since I have no son, nor will I ever have one now . . ."

His voice trailed off and he stared into the distance with unseeing eyes. It was the only time he alluded even faintly to her mother's death.

From then on, Kaede's father taught her everything that she would have learned already had she been born male. Ayame disapproved strongly—so did most of the household and the men, especially Shoji—but Kaede ignored them. She learned quickly, though much of what she learned filled her with despair.

"All Father tells me is why men rule the world," she complained to Shizuka. "Every text, every law, explains and justifies their domination."

"That is the way of the world," Shizuka replied. It was night and they lay side by side, whispering. Ai, Hana, and the other women were asleep in the adjoining room. The night was still, the air cold.

"Not everyone believes that. Maybe there are other countries where they think differently. Even here there are people who dare to think in other ways. Lady Maruyama, for instance . . ." Kaede's voice went even quieter. "The Hidden . . ."

"What do you know about the Hidden?" Shizuka said, laughing softly.

"You told me about them, a long time ago, when you first came to me at Noguchi Castle. You said they believed everyone was created equal by their god. I remember that I thought you, and they, must have been mad. But now when I learn that even the Enlightened One speaks badly of women—or at least his priests and monks do—it makes me question why it should be so."

"What do you expect?" Shizuka said. "It's men who write histories and sacred texts—even poetry. You can't change the way the world is. You have to learn how to work within it."

"There are women writers," Kaede said. "I remember hearing their tales at Noguchi Castle. But Father says I should not read them, that they will corrupt my mind."

Sometimes she thought her father selected works for her to read simply because they said such harsh things about women, and then she thought perhaps there were no other works. She particularly disliked K'ung Fu-Tzu, whom her father admired intensely. She was writing the thoughts of the sage to her father's dictation one afternoon, when a visitor arrived.

The weather had changed in the night. The air was damp with a cold edge to it. Wood smoke and mist hung together in the valleys. In the garden the heavy heads of the last chrysanthemums drooped with moisture. The women had spent the last weeks preparing the winter clothes, and Kaede was grateful for the quilted garments she now wore under her robes. Sitting writing and reading made her hands and feet cold. Soon she would have to arrange for braziers: She feared the onset of winter for which they were still so unprepared.

Ayame came bustling to the door and said in a voice tinged with alarm, "Lord Fujiwara is here, sir."

Kaede said, "I will leave you," placed the brush down, and stood.

"No, stay. It will amuse him to meet you. No doubt he's come to hear whatever news you may have brought from the East."

Her father went to the doorway and stepped out to welcome his guest. He turned and beckoned to Kaede and then dropped to his knees.

The courtyard was filled with men on horseback and other attendants. Lord Fujiwara was descending from a palanquin that had been set down beside the huge flat rock that had been transported to the garden expressly for that purpose; Kaede remembered the day from her childhood. She marveled briefly that anyone should so travel by choice, and hoped guiltily that the men had brought their own food with them. Then she dropped to her knees as one of the attendants loosened the nobleman's sandals and he stepped out of them and into the house.

She managed to look at him before she cast her eyes downward. He was tall and slender, his face white and sculpted like a mask, the forehead abnormally high. His clothes were subdued in color, but elegant and made of exquisite fabric.

He gave out a seductive fragrance that suggested boldness and originality. He returned her father's bow graciously and responded to his greeting in courteous, flowery language.

Kaede remained motionless as he stepped past her into the room, the scent filling her nostrils.

"My eldest daughter," her father said casually as he followed his guest inside. "Otori Kaede."

"Lady Otori," she heard him say, and then: "I would like to look at her."

"Come in, daughter," her father said impatiently, and she went in on her knees.

"Lord Fujiwara," she murmured.

"She is very beautiful," the nobleman remarked. "Let me see her face."

She raised her eyes and met his gaze.

"Exquisite."

In his narrowed appraising eyes she saw admiration but no desire. It surprised her, and she smiled slightly but unguardedly. He seemed equally surprised, and the sternly held line of his lips softened.

"I am disturbing you," he apologized, his glance taking in the writing instruments and the scrolls. Curiosity got the better of him. One eyebrow went up. "A lesson?"

"It's nothing," her father replied, embarrassed. "A girl's foolishness. You will think me a very indulgent father."

"On the contrary, I am fascinated." He picked up the page she had been writing on. "May I?"

"Please, please," her father said.

"Quite a fine hand. One would not believe it to be a girl's."

Kaede felt herself blush. She was reminded again of her boldness in daring to learn men's affairs.

"Do you like K'ung Fu-Tzu?" Lord Fujiwara addressed her directly, confusing her even more.

"I'm afraid my feelings toward him are mixed," she replied. "He seems to care so little for me."

"Daughter," her father remonstrated, but Fujiwara's lips moved again into something approaching a smile.

"He cannot have anticipated such a close acquaintance," he replied lightly. "You have arrived lately from Inuyama, I believe. I must confess, my visit is partly to find out what news there is."

"I came nearly a month ago," she replied. "Not directly from Inuyama, but from Terayama, where Lord Otori is buried."

"Your husband? I had not heard. My condolences."

His glance ran over her form. *Nothing escapes him,* she thought. *He has eyes like a cormorant.*

"Iida brought about his death," she said quietly, "and was killed in turn by the Otori."

Fujiwara went on to express his sympathy further, and she spoke briefly of Arai and the situation at Inuyama, but beneath his formal elegant speech she thought she discerned a hunger to know more. It disturbed her a little, but at the same time she was tempted by it. She felt she could tell him anything and that nothing would shock him, and she was flattered by his obvious interest in her.

"This is the Arai who swore allegiance to the Noguchi," her father said, returning with anger to his main grudge. "Because of his treachery I found myself fighting men from the Seishuu clan on my own land—some of them my own relatives. I was betrayed and outnumbered."

"Father!" Kaede tried to silence him. It was none of Lord Fujiwara's concern, and the less said about the disgrace, the better.

The nobleman acknowledged the disclosure with a slight bow. "Lord Shirakawa was wounded, I believe."

"Too slightly," he replied. "Better had I been killed. I should take my own life, but my daughters weaken me."

Kaede had no desire to hear any more. Luckily they were interrupted by Ayame bringing tea and small pieces of sweetened bean paste. Kaede served the men and then excused herself, leaving them to talk further. Fujiwara's eyes followed her as she left, and she found herself hoping she might talk with him again but without her father present.

She could not suggest such a meeting directly, but from time to time she tried to think of ways to make it happen. A few days later, however, her father told her a message had come from the nobleman inviting Kaede to visit him to view his collection of paintings and other treasures.

"You have aroused his interest in some way," he said, a little surprised.

Pleased though somewhat apprehensive, Kaede told Shizuka to go to the stables and ask Amano to get Raku ready and to ride with her to Fujiwara's residence, which was a little more than an hour's journey away.

"You must go in the palanquin," Shizuka replied firmly.

"Why?"

"Lord Fujiwara is from the court. He is a nobleman. You

can't go and visit him on a horse, like a warrior." Shizuka looked stern and then spoiled the effect by giggling and adding, "Now, if you were a boy and rode up on Raku, he would probably never let you go! But you have to impress him as a woman; you must be presented perfectly." She looked critically at Kaede. "He'll think you too tall, no doubt."

"He already said I was beautiful," Kaede replied, stung.

"He needs to find you flawless, like a piece of celadon or a painting by Sesshu. Then he'll feel the desire to add you to his collection."

"I don't want to be part of his collection," she exclaimed.

"What *do* you want?" Shizuka's voice had turned serious.

Kaede answered in a similar tone. "I want to restore my land and claim what is mine. I want to have power as men have."

"Then you need an ally," Shizuka replied. "If it is to be Lord Fujiwara, you must be perfect for him. Send a message to say you had a bad dream and that the day seems inauspicious. Tell him you will attend on him the day after tomorrow. That should give us time."

The message was sent and Kaede submitted herself to Shizuka's efforts. Her hair was washed, her eyebrows plucked, her skin scrubbed with bran, massaged with lotions, and scrubbed again. Shizuka went through all the garments in the house and selected some of Kaede's mother's robes for her to wear. They were not new, but the materials were of high quality and the colors—gray like a dove's wing and the purple of bush clover—brought out Kaede's ivory skin and the blue-black lights in her hair.

"You are certainly beautiful enough to attract his interest," Shizuka said. "But you must also intrigue him. Don't tell him too much. I believe he is a man who loves secrets. If you share your secrets with him, be sure he pays a fair price for them."

The nights had turned cold with the first frosts, but the days were clear. The mountains that encircled her home were brilliant with maple and sumac, as red as flames against the dark-green cedars and the blue sky. Kaede's senses were heightened by her pregnancy, and as she stepped from the palanquin in the garden of the Fujiwara residence, the beauty before her moved her deeply. It was a perfect moment of autumn, and would so soon vanish forever, driven away by the storm winds that would come howling from the mountains.

The house was larger than her own and in much better repair. Water flowed through the garden, trickling over ancient stones and through pools where gold and red carp swam lazily. The mountains seemed to rise directly from the garden, and a distant waterfall both echoed and mirrored the stream. Two great eagles soared above in the cloudless sky.

A young man greeted her at the step and led the way across a wide veranda to the main room where Lord Fujiwara was already sitting. Kaede stepped inside the doorway and sank to her knees, touching her forehead to the floor. The matting was fresh and new, the color still pale green, the scent poignant.

Shizuka remained outside, kneeling on the wooden floor. Within the room there was silence. Kaede waited for him to speak, knowing he was studying her, trying to see as much as she could of the room without moving her eyes or her head. It was a relief when he finally addressed her and begged her to sit up.

"I am very pleased you could come," he said, and they exchanged formalities, she keeping her voice soft and low, he speaking in such flowery language that sometimes she could only guess at the meaning of the words. She hoped that, if she said as little as possible, he would find her enigmatic rather than dull.

The young man returned with tea utensils and Fujiwara

himself made tea, whisking the green powder into a foaming brew. The bowls were rough, pink brown in color, pleasing to both eye and hand. She turned hers, admiring it.

"It's from Hagi," he said. "From Lord Otori's hometown. It is my favorite of all the tea ware." After a moment he went on: "Will you go there?"

Of course, I should, Kaede thought rapidly. *If he really were my husband and I were carrying his child, I would go to his house, to his family.*

"I cannot," she said simply, raising her eyes. As always the memory of Shigeru's death and the role she had played in it and in the act of revenge brought her almost to tears, darkening her eyes, making them glow.

"There are always reasons," he said obliquely. "Take my own situation. My son, my wife's grave, are in the capital. You may not have heard this: I myself was asked to leave. My writings displeased the regent. After my exile, the city was subjected to two huge earthquakes and a series of fires. It was generally believed to be heaven's displeasure at such unjust treatment of a harmless scholar. Prayers were offered and I was begged to return, but for the time being my life here pleases me, and I find reasons not to obey immediately—though, of course, eventually I must."

"Lord Shigeru has become a god," she said. "Hundreds of people go every day to pray at his shrine, at Terayama."

"Lord Shigeru, alas for us all, is dead, however, and I am still very much alive. It is too early for me to become a god."

He had told her something of himself and now she felt moved to do the same. "His uncles wanted him dead," she said. "That is why I will not go to them."

"I know little of the Otori clan," he said, "apart from the beautiful pottery they produce in Hagi. They have the reputation of skulking there. It's quite inaccessible, I believe. And they have some ancient connection with the imperial family." His voice was light, almost bantering, but when he went on it changed slightly. The same intensity of feeling that she had noticed previously had entered it again. "Forgive me if I am intruding, but how did Lord Shigeru die?"

She had spoken so little of the terrible events at Inuyama that she longed to unburden herself to him now, but as he leaned toward her she felt his hunger again, not for her, but to know what she had suffered.

"I cannot speak of it," she said in a low voice. She would make him pay for her secrets. "It is too painful."

"Ah." Fujiwara looked down at the bowl in his hand.

Kaede allowed herself to study him, the sculpted bones of his face, the sensuous mouth, the long, delicate fingers. He placed the bowl on the matting and glanced up at her. She deliberately held his gaze, let tears form in her eyes, then looked away.

"Maybe one day . . ." she said softly.

They sat without moving or speaking for several moments.

"You intrigue me," he said finally. "Very few women do. Let me show you my humble place, my meager collection."

She placed the bowl on the floor and stood gracefully. He watched every movement she made, but with none of the predatory desire of other men. Kaede realized what Shizuka had meant: If he admired her, this nobleman would want to add her to his collection. What price would he pay for her, and what could she demand?

Shizuka bowed to the floor as they stepped past her, and the young man appeared again from the shadows. He was as fine-boned and as delicate as a girl.

"Mamoru," Fujiwara said, "Lady Otori has kindly consented to look at my pathetic pieces. Come with us."

As the young man bowed to her, Fujiwara said, "You should learn from her. Study her. She is a perfect specimen."

Kaede followed them to the center of the house, where there was a courtyard and a stage area.

"Mamoru is an actor," Fujiwara said. "He plays women's roles. I like to present dramas in this small space."

Maybe it was not large, but it was exquisite. Plain wooden pillars supported the ornately carved roof, and on the backdrop a twisted pine tree was painted.

"You must come and watch a performance," Fujiwara said. "We are about to start rehearsing *Atsumori.* We are waiting for our flute player to arrive. But before that we will present *The Fulling Block.* Mamoru can learn a lot from you, and I would like your opinion of his performance."

When she said nothing he went on, "You are familiar with drama?"

"I saw a few plays when I was at Lord Noguchi's," she replied, "but I know little about it."

"Your father told me you were a hostage with the Noguchi."

"From the age of seven."

"What curious lives women lead," he remarked, and a chill came over her.

They went from the theater to another reception room

that gave out onto a smaller garden. Sunlight streamed into it and Kaede was grateful for its warmth. But the sun was already low over the mountains. Soon their peaks would hide it, and their jagged shadows would cover the valley. She could not help shivering.

"Bring a brazier," Fujiwara ordered. "Lady Otori is cold."

Mamoru disappeared briefly and came back with a much older man who carried a small brazier glowing with charcoal.

"Sit near it," Fujiwara said. "It is easy to take a chill at this time of year."

Mamoru left the room again, never speaking, his movements graceful, deferential, and soundless. When he returned he was carrying a small paulownia-wood chest, which he set down carefully on the floor. He left the room and returned three more times, each time bringing a chest or box. Each was of a different wood, zelkova, cypress, cherry, polished so that the color and grain spoke of the long life of the tree, the slope it had grown on, the seasons of hot and cold, rain and wind, that it had endured.

Fujiwara opened them one by one. Within lay bundles, objects wrapped in several layers of cloth. The wrapping cloths themselves were beautiful, although obviously very old—silks of the finest weave and the most subtle colors—but what lay within these cloths far surpassed anything Kaede had ever seen. He unwrapped each one, placed it on the floor in front of her, and invited her to take it up, caress it with her fingers, touch it to her lips, or brow, for often the feel and the scent of the object were as important as its look. He rewrapped and replaced each one before displaying the next.

"I look at them rarely," he said, with love in his voice. "Each time an unworthy gaze falls on them it diminishes them. Just to unwrap them is an erotic act for me. To share them with another whose gaze enhances rather than diminishes is one of my greatest, but rarest, pleasures."

Kaede said nothing, knowing little of the value or tradition of the objects before her: the tea bowl of the same pink-brown pottery, at once fragile and sturdy; the jade figure of the Enlightened One, seated within the lotus; the gold lacquered box that was both simple and intricate. She simply gazed, and it seemed to her that the beautiful things had their own eyes and gazed back at her.

Mamoru did not stay to look at the objects, but after what seemed a long time—for Kaede time had stopped—he returned with a large, flat box. Fujiwara took out a painting:

a winter landscape with two crows, black against the snow, in the foreground.

"Ah, Sesshu," she whispered, speaking for the first time.

"Not Sesshu, in fact, but one of his masters," he corrected her. "It's said that the child cannot teach the parent, but in Sesshu's case we must allow that the pupil surpassed the teacher."

"Is there not a saying that the blue of the dye is deeper than the blue of the flower?" she replied.

"You approve of that, I expect."

"If neither child nor pupil were ever wiser, nothing would ever change."

"And most people would be very satisfied!"

"Only those who have power," Kaede said. "They want to hold on to their power and position, while others see that same power and desire it. It's within all men to be ambitious, and so they make change happen. The young overthrow the old."

"And is it within women to be ambitious?"

"No one bothers to ask them." Her eyes returned to the painting. "Two crows, the drake and the duck, the stag and the hind—they are always painted together, always in pairs."

"That is the way nature intends it," Fujiwara said. "It is one of K'ung Fu-Tzu's five relationships, after all."

"And the only one open to women. He only sees us as wives."

"That is what women are."

"But surely a woman could be a ruler or a friend?" Her eyes met his.

"You are very bold for a girl," he replied, the nearest she had seen him come to laughing. She flushed and looked again at the painting.

"Terayama is famous for its Sesshus," Fujiwara said. "Did you see them there?"

"Yes. Lord Otori wanted Lord Takeo to see them and copy them."

"A younger brother?"

"His adopted son." The last thing Kaede wanted to do was to talk to Fujiwara about Takeo. She tried to think of something else to say, but all thoughts deserted her, except for the memory of the painting Takeo had given her of the little mountain bird.

"I presume he carried out the revenge? He must be very courageous. I doubt my son would do as much for me."

"He was always very silent," she said, longing to talk about him, yet fearing to. "You would not think him particularly courageous. He liked drawing and painting. He turned out to be fearless." She heard her own voice and stopped abruptly, sure she was transparent to him.

"Ah," Fujiwara said, and looked at the painting again for a long time.

"I mustn't intrude on your affairs," he said finally, his eyes returning to her face. "But surely you will be married to Lord Shigeru's son."

"There are other considerations," she said, trying to speak lightly. "I have land here and at Maruyama that I must lay claim to. If I go and skulk with the Otori in Hagi, I may lose all that."

"I feel you have many secrets for someone so young," he murmured. "I hope one day to hear them."

The sun was slipping toward the mountains. The shadows from the huge cedars began to stretch out toward the house.

"It is growing late," he said. "I am sorry to lose you but feel I must send you on your way. You will come again soon." He wrapped up the painting and replaced it in its box. She could smell the faint fragrance of the wood and of the rue leaves placed inside to ward off insects.

"Thank you from my heart," she said as they rose. Mamoru had returned silently to the room and now bowed deeply as she passed by him.

"Look at her, Mamoru," Fujiwara said. "Watch how she walks, how she returns your bow. If you can capture that, you can call yourself an actor."

They exchanged farewells, Lord Fujiwara himself coming out onto the veranda to see her into the palanquin and sending retainers to accompany her.

"You did well," Shizuka told her when they were home. "You intrigued him."

"He despises me," Kaede said. She felt exhausted from the encounter.

"He despises women, but he sees you as something different."

"Something unnatural."

"Maybe," Shizuka said, laughing. "Or something unique and rare that no one else possesses."

·5·

The following day Fujiwara sent presents for her, with an invitation to attend a performance of a play at the full moon. Kaede unwrapped two robes: one old and restrained, beautifully embroidered with pheasants and autumn grasses in gold and green on ivory-colored silk; the other new, it seemed, and more flamboyant, with deep purple and blue peonies on pale pink.

Hana and Ai came to admire them. Lord Fujiwara had also sent food, quail and sweetfish, persimmons and bean cakes. Hana, like all of them always on the edge of hunger, was deeply impressed.

"Don't touch," Kaede scolded her. "Your hands are dirty."

Hana's hands were stained from gathering chestnuts, but she hated anyone reprimanding her. She pulled them behind her back and stared angrily at her older sister.

"Hana," Kaede said, trying to be gentle, "let Ayame wash your hands, then you may look."

Kaede's relationship with her younger sister was still uneasy. Privately she thought Hana had been spoiled by Ayame and Ai. She wished she could persuade her father to teach Hana, too, feeling the girl needed discipline and challenges in her life. She wanted to instill them herself, but lacked the time and the patience to do so. It was something else she would have to think about during the long winter months. Now Hana ran off to the kitchen, crying.

"I'll go to her," Ai said.

"She is so self-willed," Kaede said to Shizuka. "What is to become of her when she is so beautiful and so stubborn?"

Shizuka gave her a mocking look, but said nothing.

"What?" Kaede said. "What do you mean?"

"She is like you, lady," Shizuka murmured.

"So you said before. She is luckier than I am, though." Kaede fell silent, thinking of the difference between them. When she was Hana's age she had been alone in Noguchi

Castle for over two years. Perhaps she was jealous of her sister and it was this that made her impatient. But Hana really was running wild beyond control.

She sighed, gazing on the beautiful robes, longing to feel the softness of the silk against her skin. She told Shizuka to bring a mirror and held the older robe up to her face to see the colors against her hair. She was more impressed than she revealed by the gifts. Lord Fujiwara's interest flattered her. He had said that she intrigued him; he intrigued her no less.

She wore the older robe, for it seemed more suitable for late autumn, when she and her father, Shizuka, and Ai went to visit Lord Fujiwara for the performance. They were to stay overnight, since the drama would go on until late, under the full moon. Hana, desperate to be invited, too, sulked when they left and would not come out to say good-bye. Kaede wished she could have left her father behind, too. His unpredictable behavior worried her, and she was afraid he might shame himself further in company. But he, immensely flattered by the invitation, would not be dissuaded.

Several actors, Mamoru among them, presented *The Fulling Block.* The play disturbed Kaede deeply. During her brief visit, Mamoru had studied her more than she had realized. Now she saw herself portrayed before her eyes, saw her movements, heard her own voice sigh, *The autumn wind tells of love grown cold,* as the wife went slowly mad, waiting for her husband's return.

Brilliance of the moon, touch of the wind. The words of the chorus pierced her like a needle in her flesh. *Frost gleaming in pale light, chill the heart as the block beats and night winds moan.*

Her eyes filled with tears. All the loneliness and the longing of the woman on the stage, a woman modeled on her, seemed indeed to be hers. She had even that week helped Ayame beat their silken robes with the fulling block to soften and restore them. Her father had commented on it, saying the repetitive beat of the block was one of the most evocative sounds of autumn. The drama stripped her of her defenses. She longed for Takeo completely, achingly. If she could not have him she would die. Yet, even while her heart cracked, she remembered that she must live for the child's sake. And it seemed she felt the first tiny flutter of its watery movement within her.

Above the stage the brilliant moon of the tenth month shone coldly down. Smoke from the charcoal braziers drifted skyward. The soft beat of the drums fell into the silence. The small group watching were rapt, possessed by the beauty of the moon and the power of emotion displayed before them.

Afterward Shizuka and Ai returned to their room, but, to Kaede's surprise, Lord Fujiwara asked her to remain in the company of the men as they drank wine and ate a series of exotic dishes, mushrooms, land crabs, pickled chestnuts, and tiny squid transported in ice and straw from the coast. The actors joined them, their masks laid aside. Lord Fujiwara praised them and gave them gifts. Later, when the wine had loosened tongues and raised the level of noise, he addressed Kaede quietly.

"I am glad your father came with you. I believe he has not been well?"

"You are very kind to him," she replied. "Your understanding and consideration mean a great deal to us." She did not think it was seemly to discuss her father's state of mind with the nobleman, but Fujiwara persisted.

"Does he fall into gloomy states often?"

"He is a little unstable from time to time. My mother's death, the war . . ." Kaede looked at her father, who was talking excitedly with one of the older actors. His eyes glittered, and he did indeed look a little mad.

"I hope you will turn to me if you need help at any time."

She bowed silently, aware of the great honor he was paying her and confused by his attention. She had never sat like this in a room full of men, and felt that she should not be there, yet was unsure of how to leave. He changed the subject deftly.

"What was your opinion of Mamoru? He learned well from you, I think."

She did not answer for a moment, turning her gaze from her father to the young man, who had divested himself of his female role yet still retained the vestiges of it, of her.

"What can I say?" she said finally. "He seemed brilliant to me."

"But . . . ?" he questioned.

"You steal everything from us." She had meant to say it lightly, but her voice sounded bitter to her own ears.

"*'You'?*" he repeated, slightly surprised.

"Men. You take everything from women. Even our pain—the very pain that you cause us—you steal it and portray it as your own."

His opaque eyes searched her face. "I have never seen a more convincing or moving portrayal than Mamoru's."

"Why are women's roles not played by women?"

"What a curious idea," he replied. "You think you would have more authenticity because you imagine these emotions are familiar to you. But it is the actor's artifice in creating emotions that he cannot know intimately that displays his genius."

"You leave us nothing," Kaede said.

"We give you our children. Isn't that a fair exchange?"

Again she felt his eyes could see right through her. *I dislike him,* she thought, *even though he is intriguing. I will have nothing more to do with him, no matter what Shizuka says.*

"I have offended you," he said, as though he could read her thoughts.

"I am too insignificant for Lord Fujiwara to concern himself with," she replied. "My feelings are of no importance."

"I take great interest in your feelings: They are always so original and unexpected."

Kaede made no response. After a second he went on, "You must come and see our next play. It is to be *Atsumori.* We await only our flute player. He is a friend of Mamoru's, expected any day now. You are familiar with the story?"

"Yes," she said, her mind turning to the tragedy. She was still thinking about it later when she lay in the guest room with Ai and Shizuka: the youth so beautiful and gifted at music, the rough warrior who slays him and takes his head and then in remorse becomes a monk, seeking the peace of the Enlightened One. She thought about Atsumori's wraith, calling from the shadows: *Pray for me. Let my spirit be released.*

The unfamiliar excitement, the emotions aroused by the play, the lateness of the hour, all made her restless. Thinking about Atsumori, the flute player, she drifted between sleeping and waking, and seemed to hear the notes of a flute come from the garden. It reminded her of something. She was descending toward sleep, soothed by the music, when she remembered.

She woke instantly. It was the same music she had heard at Terayama. The young monk who had shown them the paintings—surely he had played the same notes, so laden with anguish and longing?

She pushed back the quilt and got up quietly, slid aside the paper screen, and listened. She heard a quiet knock, the scrape of the wooden door opening, Mamoru's voice, the voice of the flute player. At the end of the passage a lamp in a servant's hand briefly lit their faces. She was not dreaming. It was him.

Shizuka whispered from behind her. "Is everything all right?"

Kaede closed the screen and went to kneel beside her. "It is one of the monks from Terayama."

"Here?"

"He is the flute player they have been waiting for."

"Makoto," Shizuka said.

"I never knew his name. Will he remember me?"

"How can he forget?" Shizuka replied. "We will leave early. You must plead illness. He must not see you unexpectedly. Try and sleep for a while. I will wake you at daybreak."

Kaede lay down, but sleep was slow to come. Finally she dozed a little and woke to see daylight behind the shutters and Shizuka kneeling beside her.

She wondered if it was possible to steal away. The household was already stirring. She could hear the shutters being opened. Her father always woke early. She could not leave without at least informing him.

"Go to my father and tell him I am unwell and must go home. Ask him to make my apologies to Lord Fujiwara."

Shizuka came back after several minutes. "Lord Shirakawa is most reluctant for you to leave. He wants to know if you are well enough to go to him."

"Where is he?"

"He is in the room overlooking the garden. I have asked for tea to be brought to you. You look very pale."

"Help me dress," Kaede said. Indeed she felt faint and unwell. The tea revived her a little. Ai was awake now, lying under the quilt, her sweet-natured face pink cheeked and dark eyed from sleep, like a doll's.

"Kaede, what is it? What's the matter?"

"I am ill. I need to go home."

"I'll come with you." Ai pushed back the quilt.

"It would be better if you stayed with father," Kaede told her, "and apologize to Lord Fujiwara on my behalf."

She knelt on an impulse and stroked her sister's hair. "Stand in for me," she begged.

"I don't think Lord Fujiwara has even noticed my existence," Ai said. "It is you who have entranced him."

The caged birds in the garden were calling noisily. *He will find out my deception and never want to see me again,* Kaede thought, but it was not the nobleman's reaction that she feared: It was her father's.

"The servants told me Lord Fujiwara sleeps late," Shizuka whispered. "Go and speak to your father. I have asked for the palanquin."

Kaede nodded, saying nothing. She stepped onto the polished wood of the veranda. How beautifully the boards were laid. As she walked toward the room where her father was, scenes from the garden unfolded before her eyes: a stone lantern, framed by the last red leaves of the maple, the sun glittering on the still water of a pool, the flash of yellow and black from the long-tailed birds on their perches.

Her father sat looking out onto the garden. She could not help feeling pity for him. Lord Fujiwara's friendship meant so much to him.

In the pool a heron waited, as still as a statue.

She dropped to her knees and waited for her father to speak.

"What's this nonsense, Kaede? Your rudeness is beyond belief!"

"Forgive me, I am not well," she murmured. When he did not reply she raised her voice a little. "Father, I am unwell. I am going home now."

He still said nothing, as if ignoring her would make her go away. The heron rose with a sudden beat of wings. Two young men walked into the garden to look at the caged birds.

Kaede looked around the room, seeking a screen or something that she might hide behind, but there was nothing.

"Good morning!" her father called cheerfully.

The men turned to acknowledge him. Mamoru saw her. There was a moment when she thought he would leave the garden without approaching her, but Lord Fujiwara's treatment of her the previous night when he included her in the men's party must have emboldened him. He led the other man forward and began the formal introductions to her father. She bowed deeply, hoping to hide her face. Mamoru gave the monk's name, Kubo Makoto, and the name of the temple at Terayama. Makoto bowed, too.

"Lord Shirakawa," Mamoru said, "and his daughter, Lady Otori."

The young monk could not prevent his reaction. He turned pale and his eyes went to her face. He recognized her and spoke in the same moment.

"Lady Otori? You married Lord Takeo after all? Is he here with you?"

There was a moment of silence. Then Kaede's father spoke. "My daughter's husband was Lord Otori Shigeru."

Makoto opened his mouth as if he would deny it, thought better of it, and bowed without speaking.

Kaede's father leaned forward. "You are from Terayama? You did not know that the marriage took place there?"

Makoto said nothing. Her father spoke to her without turning his head. "Leave us alone."

She was proud of how steady her voice was when she spoke. "I am going home. Please make my apologies to Lord Fujiwara."

He made no response to her. *He will kill me,* she thought. She bowed to the two young men and saw their embarrassment and their discomfort. As she walked away, forcing herself not to hurry, not to move her head, a wave of emotion began to uncurl in her belly. She saw she would always be the object of those embarrassed looks, that scorn. She gasped at the intensity of the feeling, the sharpness of the despair that came with it. *Better to die,* she thought. *But what about my child, Takeo's child? Must it die with me?*

At the end of the veranda Shizuka was waiting for her. "We can leave now, lady. Kondo will come with us."

Kaede allowed the man to lift her into the palanquin. She was relieved to be inside, in the semidarkness where no one could see her face. *Father will never look at my face again,* she thought. *He will turn his eyes away even when he kills me.*

When she reached her house, she took off the robe that Fujiwara had given her and folded it carefully. She put on one of her mother's old robes, with a quilted garment underneath. She was cold to the bone and she did not want to tremble.

"You are back!" Hana came running into the room. "Where is Ai?"

"She stayed at Lord Fujiwara's a little longer."

"Why did you come back?" the child asked.

"I didn't feel well. I'm all right now." On an impulse Kaede said, "I'm going to give you the robe, the autumn one you liked so much. You must put it away and look after it until you are old enough to wear it."

"Don't you want it?"

"I want you to have it, and to think of me when you wear it, and pray for me."

Hana stared at her, her eyes sharp. "Where are you going?" When Kaede did not reply she went on, "Don't go away again, Older Sister."

"You won't mind," Kaede said, trying to tease her. "You won't miss me."

To her dismay, Hana began to sob noisily and then to scream. "I will miss you! Don't leave me! Don't leave me!"

Ayame came running. "Now what is it, Hana? You must not be naughty with your sister."

Shizuka came into the room. "Your father is at the ford," she said. "He has come alone, on horseback."

"Ayame," Kaede said, "take Hana out for a while. Take her to the forest. All the servants must go with you. I want no one in the house."

"But, Lady Kaede, it's so early and still so cold."

"Please do as I say," Kaede begged. Hana cried more wildly as Ayame led her away.

"It is grief that makes her so wild," Shizuka said.

"I am afraid I must inflict still more on her," Kaede exclaimed. "But she must not be here."

She stood and went to the small chest where she kept a few things. She took the knife from it, felt its weight in her forbidden left hand. Soon it would no longer matter to anyone which hand she had used.

"Which is best, in the throat or in the heart?"

"You don't have to do it," Shizuka said quietly. "We can flee. The Tribe will hide you. Think of the child."

"I can't run away!" Kaede was surprised at the loudness of her own voice.

"Then let me give you poison. It will be swift and painless. You will simply fall asleep and never—"

Kaede cut her short. "I am a warrior's daughter. I'm not afraid of dying. You know better than anyone how often I have thought of taking my own life. First I must ask Father's forgiveness, then I must use the knife on myself. My only question is, which is better?"

Shizuka came close to her. "Place the point here, at the side of your neck. Thrust it sideways and upward. That will slash the artery." Her voice, matter-of-fact to start with, faltered, and Kaede saw there were tears in her eyes. "Don't do it," Shizuka whispered. "Don't despair yet."

Kaede transferred the knife to her right hand. She heard the shouts of the guard, the horse's hoofbeats as her father rode through the gate. She heard Kondo greet him.

She gazed out onto the garden. A sudden flash of memory came to her of herself as a little child running the length of the veranda from her father to her mother and back again. *I've never remembered that before,* she thought, and whispered soundlessly, *Mother, Mother!*

Her father stepped onto the veranda. As he came through the doorway both she and Shizuka dropped to their knees, foreheads to the ground.

"Daughter," he said, his voice uncertain and thin. She looked up at him and saw his face streaked with tears, his mouth working. She had been afraid of his anger, but now she saw his madness and it frightened her more.

"Forgive me," she whispered.

"I must kill myself now." He sat heavily in front of her, taking his dagger from his belt. He looked at the blade for a long time.

"Send for Shoji," he said finally. "He must assist me. Tell your man to ride to his house and fetch him."

When she made no response, he shouted suddenly, "Tell him!"

"I'll go," Shizuka whispered. She crawled on her knees to the edge of the veranda; Kaede heard her speak to Kondo, but the man did not leave. Instead he stepped up onto the veranda and she knew he was waiting just outside the doorway.

Her father made a sudden gesture toward her. She could not help flinching, thinking he was about to hit her. He said, "There was no marriage!"

"Forgive me," she said again. "I have shamed you. I am ready to die."

"But there is a child?" He was staring at her as though she were a viper that would strike at any moment.

"Yes, there is a child."

"Who is the father? Or don't you know? Was he one of many?"

"It makes no difference now," she replied. "The child will die with me."

She thought, *Thrust the knife sideways and upward.* But she felt the child's tiny hands grip her muscles, preventing her.

"Yes, yes, you must take your own life." His voice rose, taking on a shrill energy. "Your sisters must also kill themselves. This is my last command to you. Thus the Shirakawa family will disappear, not before time. And I will not wait for Shoji. I must do it myself. It will be my final act of honor."

He loosened his sash and opened his robe, pushing aside his undergarment to expose his flesh. "Don't turn away," he said to Kaede. "You must watch. It is you who have driven me to this." He placed the point of the blade against the loose, wrinkled skin and drew a deep breath.

She could not believe it was happening. She saw his

knuckles tighten around the handle, saw his face contort. He gave a harsh cry and the dagger fell from his hands. But there was no blood, no wound. Several more sharp cries issued from him, then gave way to racking sobs.

"I cannot do it," he wailed. "My courage has all gone. You have sapped me, unnatural woman that you are. You have taken my honor and my manhood. You are not my daughter: You are a demon! You bring death to all men; you are cursed." He reached out and grabbed her, pulling at her garments. "Let me see you," he cried. "Let me see what other men desire! Bring death to me as you have to others."

"No," she screamed, fighting against his hands, trying to push him away. "Father, no!"

"You call me Father? I am not your father. My real children are the sons I never had; the sons you and your cursed sisters took the place of. Your demonic powers must have killed them in your mother's womb!" His madness gave him strength. She felt the robes pulled from her shoulders, his hands on her skin. She could not use the knife; she could not escape him. As she struggled against his grip, the robe slipped to her waist, exposing her. Her hair came loose and fell around her bare shoulders.

"You are beautiful," he shouted. "I admit it. I have desired you. While I taught you I lusted after you. It was my punishment for going against nature. I am completely corrupted by you. Now bring me death!"

"Let me go, Father," she cried, trying to stay calm, hoping to reason with him. "You are not yourself. If we must die let us do it with dignity." But all words seemed weak and meaningless in the face of his delusions.

His eyes were wet, his lips quivering. He seized her knife and threw it across the room, held both her wrists in his left hand, and pulled her toward him. With his right hand he reached under her hair, drew it aside, bent over her, and put his lips on the nape of her neck.

Horror and revulsion swept over her, followed by fury. She had been prepared to die, in accordance with the harsh code of her class, to salvage her family's honor. But her father, who had instructed her so rigidly in that code, who had taught her assiduously about the superiority of his sex, had surrendered to madness, revealing what lay beneath the strict rules of conduct of the warrior class: the lust and selfishness of men. The fury brought to life the power that she knew lay within her, and she remembered how she had slept in ice. She called to the White Goddess: *Help me!*

She heard her own voice—"Help me! Help me!"—and even as she cried out her father's grip slackened. *He has come to his senses,* she thought, pushing him away. She scrambled to her feet, pulling her robe around her and retying the sash, and, almost without thinking, stumbled to the farthest side of the room. She was sobbing with shock and rage.

She turned and saw Kondo kneeling in front of her father, who sat half-upright, supported, she thought at first, by Shizuka. Then she realized that her father's eyes saw nothing. Kondo plunged his hand, it seemed, into her father's belly and slashed crossways. The cut made a foul soft noise, and the blood hissed and bubbled as it foamed out.

Shizuka let go of the man's neck, and he fell forward. Kondo placed the knife in his right hand.

The vomit rose in her throat then and she doubled up, retching. Shizuka came to her, her face expressionless. "It's all over."

"Lord Shirakawa lost his mind," Kondo said, "and took his own life. He has had many episodes of madness and often spoke of so doing. He died honorably and with great courage." He stood and looked directly at her. There was a moment when she could have called for the guards, denounced both of them, and had them executed, but the moment passed and she did nothing. She knew she would never reveal the murder to anyone.

Kondo smiled very slightly and continued, "Lady Otori, you must demand allegiance from the men. You must be strong. Otherwise any one of them will seize your domain and usurp you."

"I was about to kill myself," she said slowly. "But it seems there is no need now."

"No need," he agreed, "as long as you are strong."

"You must live for the child's sake," Shizuka urged her. "No one will care who the father is, if only you are powerful enough. But you must act now. Kondo, summon the men as quickly as possible."

Kaede let Shizuka lead her to the women's rooms, wash her, and change her clothes. Her mind was quivering with shock, but she clung to the knowledge of her own power. Her father was dead and she was alive. He had wanted to die; it was no hardship for her to pretend that he had indeed taken his own life and had died with honor, a desire he had often expressed. Indeed, she thought bitterly, she was respecting his wishes and protecting his name. She would not, however, obey his last command to her: She would not kill herself and she would not allow her sisters to die either.

Kondo had summoned the guards, and boys were sent to the village to fetch the men who lived on farms. Within the hour, most of her father's retainers were assembled. The women had brought out the mourning clothes so recently put away after her mother's death, and the priest had been sent for. The sun came up higher, melting the frost. The air smelled of smoke and pine needles. Now that the first shock was over Kaede was driven by a feeling she hardly understood, a fierce need to secure what was hers, to protect her sisters and her household, to ensure nothing of hers was lost or stolen. Any one of the men could take her estate from her; they would not hesitate if she showed the slightest sign of weakness. She had seen the utter ruthlessness that lay beneath Shizuka's light-hearted pose and Kondo's ironic exterior. That ruthlessness had saved her life, and she would match it with her own.

She recalled the decisiveness that she had seen in Arai, that made men follow him, that had brought most of the Three Countries under his sway. She must now show the same resolution. Arai would respect their alliance, but if anyone else took her place, would he hold back from war? She would not let her people be devastated; she would not let her sisters be taken away as hostages.

Death still beckoned her, but this new fierce spirit within her would not allow her to respond. *I am indeed possessed,* she thought as she stepped onto the veranda to speak to the men assembled in the garden. *How few they are,* she thought, remembering the numbers her father used to command when she was a child. Ten were Arai's men, whom Kondo had selected, and there were twenty or so who still served the Shirakawa. She knew them all by name, had made it her business since she returned to get to know their position and something of their character.

Shoji had been one of the first to arrive and had prostrated himself before her father's body. His face still bore the traces of tears. He stood at her right hand, Kondo on her left. She was aware of Kondo's deference to the older man and aware that it was a pretense, like most of what he did. *But he killed my father for me,* she thought. *He is bound to me now. But what price will he exact in return?*

The men knelt before her, heads lowered, then sat back on their heels as she spoke.

"Lord Shirakawa has taken his own life," she said. "It was his choice, and whatever my grief, I must respect and honor his deed. My father intended me to be his heir. It was for that purpose that he began instructing me as if I were his son. I mean to carry out his wishes." She paused for a moment, hearing his final words to her, so different: *I am completely corrupted by you. Now bring me death!* But she did not flinch. To the watching men she seemed to radiate some deep power. It illuminated her eyes and made her voice irresistible. "I ask my father's men to swear allegiance to me as you did to him. Since Lord Arai and I are in alliance, I expect those of you who serve him to continue to serve me. In return I offer you both protection and advancement. I plan to consolidate Shirakawa and next year take up the lands willed to me at Maruyama. My father will be buried tomorrow."

Shoji was the first to kneel before her. Kondo followed, though again his demeanor unnerved her. *He is playacting,* she thought. *Allegiance means nothing to him. He is from the Tribe. What schemes do they have for me that I know nothing about? Can I trust them? If I find I cannot trust Shizuka, what will I do?*

Her heart quailed within her, though none of the men filing before her would have guessed. She received their allegiance, noting each one, picking out their characteristics, their clothes, armor, and weapons. They were mostly ill-equipped, the laces of the armor broken and frayed, the helmets dented and cracked, but they all had bows and swords, and she knew most of them had horses.

All knelt to her save two. One, a giant of a man, Hirogawa, called out in a loud voice, "All respect to your ladyship, but I've never served a woman and I'm too old to start now." He made a perfunctory bow and walked to the gate with a swagger that infuriated her. A smaller man, Nakao, followed him without a word, without even bowing.

Kondo looked at her. "Lady Otori?"

"Kill them," she said, knowing she had to be ruthless and knowing she had to start now.

He moved faster than she would have thought possible, cutting down Nakao before the man realized what was happening. Hirogawa turned in the gateway and drew his sword.

"You have broken your allegiance and must die," Kondo shouted at him.

The large man laughed. "You are not even from Shirakawa. Who's going to take any notice of you?" He held his sword in both hands, ready to strike. Kondo took a quick step forward; as Hirogawa's blow fell Kondo parried it with his own sword, thrusting the other man's blade aside with unexpected strength, wielding his own weapon like an ax. In the return motion he whipped it back into Hirogawa's unprotected belly. Now more like a razor than an ax, the sword slid through the flesh. As Hirogawa faltered forward Kondo stepped out to the right and behind him. Spinning round he struck downward, opening the man's back from shoulder to hip.

Kondo did not look at the dying men but turned to face the others. He said, "I serve Lady Otori Kaede, heir to Shirakawa and Maruyama. Is there anyone else here who will not serve her as faithfully as I?"

No one moved. Kaede thought she saw anger in Shoji's face, but he simply pressed his lips together, saying nothing.

In recognition of their past service to her father, she allowed the families of the dead men to collect the bodies and bury them, but because the men had disobeyed her she told Kondo to turn their dependents out of their homes and take their land for herself.

"It was the only thing to do," Shizuka told her. "If you

had allowed them to live, they would have caused unrest here or joined your enemies."

"Who are my enemies?" Kaede said. It was late in the evening. They sat in Kaede's favorite room. The shutters were closed but the braziers hardly warmed the chill night air. She pulled the quilted robes more closely around her. From the main room came the chanting of priests keeping vigil with the dead man.

"Lady Maruyama's stepdaughter is married to a cousin of Lord Iida, Nariaki. They will be your main rivals in claiming the domain."

"But most of the Seishuu hate the Tohan," Kaede replied. "I believe I will be welcomed by them. I am the rightful heir, after all, the closest blood relative to Lady Maruyama."

"No one's questioning your legal right," Shizuka replied, "but you will have to fight to obtain your inheritance. Would you not be content with your own domain here at Shirakawa?"

"The men I have are so few, and pitifully equipped," Kaede said thoughtfully. "Just to hold Shirakawa, I will need a small army. I cannot afford one with the resources we have here. I will need the wealth of Maruyama. When the mourning period is over, you must send someone to Lady Naomi's chief retainer, Sugita Haruki. You know who he is; we met him on our journey to Tsuwano. Let us hope he is still in charge of the domain."

"I must send someone?"

"You or Kondo. One of your spies."

"You want to employ the Tribe?" Shizuka said in surprise.

"I already employ you," Kaede replied. "Now I want to make use of your skills." She wanted to question Shizuka closely about many things, but she was exhausted, with an oppressive feeling in her belly and womb. *In the next day or so I will talk to her,* she promised herself, *but now I must lie down.*

Her back ached; when she was finally in bed she could not get comfortable, and sleep would not come. She had gone through the whole terrible day and she was still alive, but now that the house was quiet, the weeping and chanting stilled, a deep sense of dread came over her. Her father's words rang in her ears. His face and the faces of the dead men loomed before her eyes. She feared their ghosts would try to snatch Takeo's child from her. Finally she slept, her arms wrapped around her belly.

She dreamed her father was attacking her. He drew the

dagger from his belt but instead of plunging it into his own belly he came close to her, put his hand on the back of her neck, and drove the dagger deep into her. An agonizing pain swept through her, making her wake with a cry. The pain surged again rhythmically. Her legs were already awash with blood.

Her father's funeral took place without her. The child slipped from her womb like an eel, and her life's blood followed. Then fever came, turning her vision red, setting her tongue babbling, tormenting her with hideous visions.

Shizuka and Ayame brewed all the herbs known to them, then in despair burned incense and struck gongs to banish the evil spirits that possessed her, and called for priests and a spirit girl to drive them away.

After three days it seemed nothing would save her. Ai never left her side. Even Hana was beyond tears. Around the hour of the Goat, Shizuka stepped outside to fetch fresh water, when one of the men at the guardhouse called to her.

"Visitors are coming. Men on horses and two palanquins. Lord Fujiwara, I think."

"He must not come in," she said. "There is pollution by blood as well as by death."

The bearers set the palanquins down outside the gate, and she dropped to her knees as Fujiwara looked out.

"Lord Fujiwara, forgive me. It is impossible for you to come in."

"I was told Lady Otori is gravely ill," he replied. "Let me talk to you in the garden."

She remained kneeling as he walked past her, then rose and followed him to the pavilion by the stream. He waved his servants away and turned to Shizuka.

"How serious is it?"

"I do not think she will live beyond tonight," Shizuka replied in a low voice. "We have tried everything."

"I have brought my physician," Fujiwara said. "Show him where to go and then come back to me."

She bowed to him and went back to the gate, where the physician, a small, middle-aged man with a kind, intelligent look about him, was emerging from the second palanquin. She took him to the room where Kaede lay, her heart sinking at the sight of her pale skin and unfocused eyes. Kaede's breathing was rapid and shallow, and every now and then she gave a sharp cry—whether of fear or pain, it was impossible to tell.

When she came back Lord Fujiwara was standing gazing

toward the end of the garden, where the stream fell away over rocks. The air was beginning to chill, and the sound of the waterfall was bleak and lonely. Shizuka knelt again and waited for him to speak.

"Ishida is very skilled," he said. "Don't give up hope yet."

"Lord Fujiwara's kindness is extreme," she murmured. She could only think of Kaede's pale face and wild eyes. She longed to return to her, but she could not leave without the nobleman's permission.

"I am not a kind man," he replied. "I am motivated mainly by my own desires, by selfishness. It is my nature to be cruel." He glanced briefly at her and said, "How long have you served Lady Shirakawa? You are not from this part of the country?"

"I was sent to her in the spring while she was still at Noguchi Castle."

"Sent by whom?"

"By Lord Arai."

"Indeed? And do you report back to him?"

"What can Lord Fujiwara mean?" Shizuka said.

"There is something about you that is unusual in a servant. I wondered if you might be a spy."

"Lord Fujiwara has too high an opinion of my abilities," Shizuka replied.

"I hope you never have cause to incite my cruelty."

She heard the threat behind his words and said nothing.

He went on as if talking to himself. "Her person, her life, touch me in a way I have never felt before. I thought myself long past experiencing any new emotion. I will not let anyone or anything—even death—take her from me."

"Everyone who sees her is bewitched by her," Shizuka whispered, "but fate has been unusually harsh to her."

"I wish I knew her true life," he said. "I know she has many secrets. The recent tragedy of her father's death is another, I suppose. I hope you will tell me one day, if she cannot." His voice broke. "The idea that such beauty might perish pierces my soul," he said. Shizuka thought she heard artificiality in his voice, but his eyes were filled with tears. "If she lives I will marry her," he said. "That way I will have her with me always. You may go now. But will you tell her that?"

"Lord Fujiwara." Shizuka touched her forehead to the ground and crept away backward.

If she lives . . .

ACKNOWLEDGMENTS

I would like to thank the Asialink Foundation and all my friends in Japan and Australia who have helped me in researching and writing Tales of the Otori.

In *Grass for His Pillow* I particularly want to thank Ms. Sugiyama Kazuko for her calligraphy and Simon Higgins for his advice on martial arts.

TURN THE PAGE FOR A PREVIEW OF

Grass for His Pillow

THE WAY THROUGH THE SNOW

·1·

Matsue was a northern town, cold and austere. We arrived in the middle of autumn, when the wind from the mainland howled across a sea as dark as iron. Once the snows began, like Hagi, Matsue would be cut off from the rest of the country for three months. It was as good a place as any to learn what I had to learn.

For a week we had walked all day, following the coastal road. It did not rain, but the sky was often overcast and each day was shorter and colder than the last. We stopped at many villages and showed the children juggling, spinning tops, and games with string that Yuki and Keiko knew. At night we always found shelter with merchants who were part of the

Tribe network. I lay awake till late listening to whispered conversations, my nostrils filled with the smells of the brewery or of soybean foodstuff. I dreamed of Kaede, and longed for her, and sometimes when I was alone I would take out Shigeru's letter and read his last words, in which he had charged me to avenge his death and to take care of Lady Shirakawa. Consciously I had made the decision to go to the Tribe, but, even in those early days, just before sleep, unbidden images came to me of his uncles, unpunished in Hagi, and of his sword, Jato, sleeping at Terayama.

By the time we arrived at Matsue, Yuki and I were lovers. It happened with inevitability, yet not through my will. I was always aware of her on the road, my senses tuned to her voice, her scent. But I was too unsure of my future, my position in the group, too guarded and wary to make any move toward her. It was obvious that Akio also found her attractive. He was at ease with her as with no one else, seeking out her company, walking beside her on the road, sitting next to her at meals. I did not want to antagonize him further.

Yuki's position in the group was unclear. She deferred to Akio and always treated him with respect; yet, she seemed equal to him in status and, as I had reason to know, her skills were greater. Keiko was obviously lower down in the order, perhaps from a lesser family or a collateral branch. She continued to ignore me, but showed blind loyalty to Akio. As for the older man, Kazuo, everyone treated him as a mixture between a servant and an uncle. He had many practical skills, including thievery.

Akio was Kikuta through both father and mother. He was a second cousin to me and had the same hands shaped like mine. His physical skills were astounding—he had the fastest reflexes of anyone I've ever met, and could leap so high he seemed to be flying—but apart from his ability to perceive the use of invisibility and the second self, and his dexterity in juggling, none of the more unusual Kikuta gifts had come to him. Yuki told me this one day when we were walking some way ahead of the others.

"The masters fear the gifts are dying out. Every generation seems to have fewer." She gave me a sideways look and added, "That's why it's so important to us to keep you."

Her mother had said the same thing and I would have liked to have heard more, but Akio shouted at me that it was my turn to push the cart. I saw the jealousy in his face as I walked toward him. I understood it and his hostility to me all too well. He was fanatically loyal to the Tribe, having been raised in their teachings and way of life; I could not help but realize that my sudden appearance was likely to usurp many of his ambitions and hopes. But understanding his antipathy did not make it any easier to bear, nor did it make me like him.

I said nothing as I took the handles of the cart from him. He ran forward to walk beside Yuki, whispering to her, forgetting, as he often did, that I could hear every word. He'd taken to calling me the Dog, and the nickname had enough truth in it to stick. As I've said before, I have an affinity with dogs: I can hear the things they hear, and I've known what it's like to be speechless.

"What were you saying to the Dog?" he asked her.

"Teaching, teaching," she replied offhandedly. "There's so much he needs to learn."

But what she turned out to be best at teaching was the art of love.

Both Yuki and Keiko took on the role of prostitutes on the road if they needed to. So did many of the Tribe, men and women, no one thinking any the worse of them for it. It was simply another role to assume, then discard. Of course, the clans had quite different ideas about the virginity of their brides and the fidelity of their wives. Men could do what they liked; women were expected to be chaste. The teachings I had grown up with were somewhere between the two: The Hidden are supposed to be pure in matters of physical desire, but in practice are forgiving of one another's lapses, as they are in all things.

On our fourth night we stayed in a large village with a wealthy family. Despite the scarcity in the whole area following the storms, they had stockpiles of supplies and they were generous hosts. The merchant offered us women, maids from his household, and Akio and Kazuo accepted. I made an excuse of some sort, which brought a storm of teasing, but the matter was not forced. Later, when the girls came to the room and lay down with the other men, I moved my mattress outside onto the veranda and shivered under the brittle ice points of the stars. Desire, longing for Kaede—to be honest, at that moment for any woman—tormented me. The door slid open, and one of the girls from the household, I thought, came out onto the veranda. As she closed the door behind her, I caught her fragrance and recognized her tread.

Yuki knelt beside me. I reached out for her and pulled her down next to me. Her girdle was already undone, her robe loose. I remember feeling the most immense gratitude to her. She loosened my clothes, making it all so easy for me—too easy; I was too quick. She scolded me for my impatience, promising to teach me. And so she did.

The next morning Akio looked at me searchingly. "You changed your mind last night?"

I wondered how he knew—if he had heard us through the flimsy screens or if he was just guessing.

"One of the girls came to me. It seemed impolite to turn her away," I replied.

He grunted and did not pursue the matter, but he watched Yuki and me carefully, even though we said nothing to each other, as though he knew something had changed between us. I thought about her constantly, swinging between elation and despair: elation because the act of love with her was indescribably wonderful; despair because she was not Kaede, and because what we did together bound me ever more closely to the Tribe.

I couldn't help remembering Kenji's comment as he left: *It's a good thing Yuki's going to be around to keep an eye on you.* He had known this would happen. Had he planned it with her, instructed her? Did Akio of course know, because he had been told? I was filled with misgivings, and I did not trust Yuki, but it didn't stop me from going to her every time I had the chance. She, so much wiser in these matters, made sure the chance arose often. And Akio's jealousy grew more apparent every day.

So our little group came to Matsue, outwardly united and in harmony, but in fact torn by intense emotions that, being true members of the Tribe, we concealed from outsiders and from one another.

We stayed at the Kikuta house, another merchant's place, smelling of fermenting soybeans, paste, and sauce. The owner, Gosaburo, was Kotaro's youngest brother, also first cousin to my father. There was little need for secrecy. We were now well beyond the Three Countries and Arai's reach, and in Matsue the local clan, the Yoshida, had no quarrel with the Tribe, finding them equally useful for moneylending, spying, and assassination. Here we had news of Arai, who was busy subduing the East and the Middle Country, making alliances, fighting border skirmishes, and setting up his administration. We heard the first rumors of his campaign against the Tribe and his intention to clear his lands of them, rumors that were the source of much mirth and derision.

I will not set down the details of my training. Its aim was to harden my heart and instill in me ruthlessness. But even now, years later, the memory of its harshness and cruelty makes me flinch and want to turn my eyes away. They were cruel times: Maybe Heaven was angry, maybe men were taken over by devils, maybe when the powers of good weaken, the brutal, with its nose for rot, storms in. The Tribe, cruelest of the cruel, flourished.

I was not the only Tribe member in training. There were several other boys, most of them much younger, all of them born Kikuta and raised in the family. The one closest to me in age was a solidly built, cheerful-faced young man with whom I was often paired. His name was Hajime, and though he did not exactly deflect Akio's rage toward me—to do so openly would be unthinkably disobedient—he often managed to draw some of it away. There was something about him I liked, though I would not go as far as to say I trusted him. His fighting skills were far greater than mine. He was a wrestler, and also strong enough to pull the huge bows of the master archers, but in the skills that are given rather than learned, neither he nor any of the others came near what I could do. It was only now that I began to realize how exceptional these skills were. I could go invisible for minutes on end, even in the bare white-walled hall; sometimes not even Akio could see me. I could split myself while fighting and watch my opponent grapple with my second self from the other side of the room. I could move without sound while my own hearing became ever more acute, and the younger boys quickly learned never to look me directly in the eye. I had put all of them to sleep at one time or another. I was learning slowly to control this skill as I practiced on them. When I looked into their eyes I saw the weaknesses and fears that made them vulnerable to my gaze: sometimes their own inner fears, sometimes fear of me and the uncanny powers that had been given to me.

Every morning I did exercises with Akio to build up strength and speed. I was slower and weaker than he was in almost all areas, and he had gained nothing in patience. But to give him his due, he was determined to teach me some of his skills in leaping and flying, and he succeeded. Part of those skills were in me already—my stepfather, after all, used to call me a wild monkey—and Akio's brutal but skillful teaching drew them to the surface and showed me how to control them. After only a few weeks I was aware of the difference in me, of how much I had hardened in mind and body.

We always finished with fighting bare-handed—not that the Tribe used this art much, preferring assassination to actual combat—but we were all trained in it. Then we sat in silent meditation, a robe slung across our cooling bodies, keeping our body temperature up by force of will. My head was usually ringing from some blow or fall, and I did not empty my mind as I was supposed to but instead dwelt savagely on how I would like to see Akio suffer. I gave to him all of Jo-An's torment that he'd once described to me.

My training was designed to encourage cruelty, and I embraced it at the time wholeheartedly, glad for the skills it was giving me, delighted at how they enhanced those I had learned with the Otori warriors' sons back when Shigeru was still alive. My father's Kikuta blood came to life in me. My mother's compassion drained away, along with all the teachings of my childhood. I no longer prayed; neither the Secret God, nor the Enlightened One, nor the old spirits meant anything to me. I did not believe in their existence and I saw no evidence that they favored those who did. Sometimes in the night I would wake suddenly and catch an unprotected glimpse of myself, and shudder at what I was becoming, and then I would rise silently and, if I could, go and find Yuki, lie down with her, and lose myself in her.

We never spent the whole night together. Our encounters were always short and usually silent. But one afternoon we found ourselves alone in the house, apart from the servants who were occupied in the shop. Akio and Hajime had taken the younger boys to the shrine for some dedication ceremony, and I had been told to copy some documents for Gosaburo. I was grateful for the task. I rarely held a brush in my hands, and because I had learned to write so late, I was always afraid the characters would desert me. The merchant had a few books and, as Shigeru had instructed me, I read whenever I could, but I had lost my inkstone and brushes at Inuyama and had hardly written since.

I diligently copied the documents—records from the shop, accounts of the amount of soybeans and rice purchased from local farmers—but my fingers were itching to draw. I was reminded of my first visit to Terayama, the brilliance of the summer day, the beauty of the paintings, the little mountain bird I had drawn and given to Kaede.

As always, when I was thinking of the past, my heart unguarded, she came to me and took possession of me all over again. I could feel her presence, smell the fragrance of her hair, hear her voice. So strongly was she with me, I had a moment of fear, as if her ghost had slipped into the room. Her ghost would be angry with me, filled with resentment and rage for abandoning her. Her words rang in my ears: *I'm afraid of myself. I only feel safe with you.*

It was cold in the room and already growing dark, with all the threat of the winter to come. I shivered, full of remorse and regret. My hands were numb with cold.

I could hear Yuki's footsteps approaching from the back of the building. I started writing again. She crossed the courtyard and stepped out of her sandals onto the veranda of the records room. I could smell burning charcoal. She had brought a small brazier, which she placed on the floor next to me.

"You look cold," she said. "Shall I bring tea?"

"Later, maybe." I laid down the brush and held my hands out to the warmth. She took them and rubbed them between her own.

"I'll close the shutters," she said.

"Then you'll have to bring a lamp. I can't see to write."

She laughed quietly. The wooden shutters slid into place, one after another. The room went dim, lit only by the faint glow of the charcoal. When Yuki came back to me she had already loosened her robe. Soon we were both warm. But after the act of love, as wonderful as ever, my unease returned. Kaede's spirit had been in the room with me. Was I causing her anguish and arousing her jealousy and spite?

Curled against me, the heat radiating from her, Yuki said, "A message came from your cousin."

"Which cousin?" I had dozens of them now.

"Muto Shizuka."

I eased myself away from Yuki so she would not hear the quickened beating of my heart. "What did she say?"

"Lady Shirakawa is dying. Shizuka said she feared the end was very near." Yuki added in her indolent, sated voice, "Poor thing."

She was glowing with life and pleasure. But the only thing I was aware of in the room was Kaede, her frailty, her intensity, her supernatural beauty. I called out to her in my soul: *You cannot die. I must see you again. I will come for you. Don't die before I see you again!*

Her spirit gazed on me, her eyes dark with reproach and sorrow.

Yuki turned and looked up at me, surprised by my

silence. "Shizuka thought you should know: Was there something between you? My father hinted as much, but he said it was just green love. He said everyone who saw her became infatuated with her."

I did not answer. Yuki sat up, pulling her robe around her. "It was more than that, wasn't it? You loved her." She seized my hands and turned me to face her. "You loved her," she repeated, the jealousy beginning to show in her voice. "Is it over?"

"It will never be over," I said. "Even if she dies I can never stop loving her." Now that it was too late to tell Kaede, I knew that it was true.

"That part of your life is finished," Yuki said quietly but fiercely. "All of it. Forget her! You will never see her again." I could hear the anger and frustration in her voice.

"I would never have told you if you had not mentioned her." I pulled my hands away from her and dressed again. The warmth had gone from me as swiftly as it had come. The brazier was cooling.

"Bring some more charcoal," I told Yuki. "And lamps. I must finish the work."

"Takeo—" she began, and then broke off abruptly. "I'll

send the maid," she said, getting to her feet. She touched the back of my neck as she left, but I made no response. Physically we had been deeply involved: Her hands had massaged me, and struck me in punishment. We had killed side by side; we had made love. But she had barely brushed the surface of my heart, and at that moment we both knew it.

I made no sign of my grief, but I wept inwardly for Kaede and for the life that we might have had together. No further word came from Shizuka, though I never stopped listening for messengers. Yuki did not mention the subject again. I could not believe Kaede was dead, and in the daytime I clung to that belief, but the nights were different.

The last of the color faded as leaves fell from maple and willow. Strings of wild geese flew southward across the sullen sky. Messengers became less frequent as the town began to close down for winter. But they still came from time to time, bringing news of Tribe activities and of the fighting in the Three Countries, and, always, bringing new orders for our trade.

For that was how we described our work of spying and killing: trade, with human lives measured out as so many units. I copied records of these, too, often sitting till late into the night with Gosaburo, the merchant, moving from the soybean harvest to the other, deadlier one. Both showed a fine profit, though the soybeans had been affected by the storms while the murders had not, though one candidate for assassination had drowned before the Tribe could get to him and there was an ongoing dispute about payment.

The Kikuta, being more ruthless, were supposed to be more skilled at assassination than the Muto, who were traditionally the most effective spies. These two families were the aristocracy of the Tribe; the other three, Kuroda, Kudo, and Imai, worked at more menial and humdrum tasks, being servants, petty thieves, informants, and so on. Because the traditional skills were so valued, there were many marriages between Muto and Kikuta, fewer between them and the other families, though the exceptions often threw up geniuses like the assassin Shintaro.

After dealing with the accounts, Kikuta Gosaburo would give me lessons in genealogy, explaining the intricate relationships of the Tribe that spread like an autumn spider's web across the Three Countries, into the North and beyond. He was a fat man with a double chin like a woman's and a smooth, plump face, deceptively gentle-looking. The smell of fermentation clung to his clothes and skin. If he was in a good mood he would call for wine and move from genealogy into history—the Tribe history of my ancestors. Little had changed in hundreds of years. Warlords might rise and fall, clans flourish and disappear, but the trade of the Tribe in all the essentials of life went on forever. Except now Arai wanted to bring about change. All other powerful warlords worked with the Tribe. Only Arai wanted to destroy them.

Gosaburo's chins wobbled with laughter at the idea.

At first I was called on only as a spy, sent to overhear conversations in taverns and teahouses, ordered to climb over walls and roofs at night and listen to men confiding in their sons or their wives. I heard the townspeople's secrets and fears, the Yoshida clan's strategies for spring, the concerns at the castle about Arai's intentions beyond the borders and about peasant uprisings close to home. I went into the mountain villages, listened to those peasants, and identified the ringleaders.

One night Gosaburo clicked his tongue in disapproval at a long-overdue account. Not only had no payments been made, more goods had been ordered. The man's name was

Furoda, a low-ranking warrior who had turned to farming to support his large family and his liking for the good things in life. Beneath his name I read the symbols that indicated the rising level of intimidation already used against him: A barn had been set alight, one of his daughters abducted, a son beaten up, dogs and horses killed. Yet, he still sank ever more deeply into the Kikuta's debt.

"This could be one for the Dog," the merchant said to Akio, who had joined us for a glass of wine. Like everyone except Yuki, he used Akio's nickname for me.

Akio took the scroll and ran his eyes over Furoda's sad history. "He's had a lot of leeway."

"Well, he's a likable fellow. I've known him since we were boys. I can't go on making allowances for him, though."

"Uncle, if you don't deal with him, isn't everyone going to expect the same leniency?" Akio said.

"That's the trouble: No one's paying on time at the moment. They all think they can get away with it because Furoda has." Gosaburo sighed deeply, his eyes almost disappearing in the folds of his cheeks. "I'm too softhearted. That's my problem. My brothers are always telling me."

"The Dog is softhearted," Akio said. "But we're training

him not to be. He can take care of Furoda for you. It will be good for him."

"If you kill him he can never pay his debts," I said.

"But everyone else will." Akio spoke as if pointing out an obvious truth to a simpleton.

"It's often easier to claim from a dead man than a live one," Gosaburo added apologetically.

I did not know this easygoing, pleasure-loving, irresponsible man, and I did not want to kill him. But I did. A few days later I went at night to his house on the outskirts of town, silenced the dogs, went invisible, and slipped past the guards. The house was well barred but I waited for him outside the privy. I had been watching the house and I knew he always rose in the early hours to relieve himself. He was a large, fleshy man who'd long since given up any training and who had handed over the heavy work on the land to his sons. He'd grown soft. He died with hardly a sound.

When I untwisted the garrote, rain had started to fall. The tiles of the walls were slippery. The night was at its darkest. The rain could almost be sleet. I returned to the Kikuta house silenced by the darkness and the cold as if they had crept inside me and left a shadow on my soul.

Furoda's sons paid his debts, and Gosaburo was pleased with me. I let no one see how much the murder had disturbed me, but the next one was worse. It was on the orders of the Yoshida family. Determined to put a stop to the unrest among the villagers before winter, they put in a request for the leader to be eradicated. I knew the man, knew his secret fields, though I had not yet revealed them to anyone. Now I told Gosaburo and Akio where he could be found alone every evening, and they sent me to meet him there.

He had rice and sweet potatoes concealed in a small cave, cut into the side of the mountain and covered with stones and brushwood. He was working on the banks of the field when I came silently up the slope. I'd misjudged him: He was stronger than I thought, and he fought back with his hoe. As we struggled together, my hood slipped back and he saw my face. Recognition came into his eyes, mixed with a sort of horror. In that moment I used my second self, came behind him, and cut his throat, but I'd heard him call out to my image.

"Lord Shigeru!"

I was covered with blood, his and mine, and dizzy from the blow I'd not quite avoided. The hoe had glanced against my scalp and the scrape was bleeding freely. His words disturbed me deeply. Had he been calling to Shigeru's spirit for help, or had he seen my likeness and mistaken me for him? I wanted to question him, but his eyes stared blankly up at the twilight sky. He was beyond speech forever.

I went invisible and stayed so until I was nearly back at the Kikuta house, the longest period I had ever used it for. I would have stayed like that forever if I could. I could not forget the man's last words, and then I remembered what Shigeru had said, so long ago, in Hagi: *I have never killed an unarmed man, nor killed for pleasure.*

The clan lords were highly satisfied. The man's death had taken the heart out of the unrest. The villagers promptly became docile and obedient. Many of them would die of starvation before the end of winter. It was an excellent result, Gosaburo said.

But I began to dream of Shigeru every night. He entered the room and stood before me as if he had just come out of the river, blood and water streaming from him, saying nothing, his eyes fixed on me as if he were waiting for me—the same way he had waited with the patience of the heron for me to speak again.

Slowly it began to dawn on me that I could not bear the life I was living, but I did not know how to escape it. I had made a bargain with the Kikuta that I was now finding impossible to keep. I'd made the bargain in the heat of passion, not expecting to live beyond that night, and with no understanding of my own self. I'd thought the Kikuta master, who seemed to know me, would help me resolve the deep divisions and contradictions of my nature, but he had sent me away to Matsue with Akio, where my life with the Tribe might be teaching me how to hide these contradictions but was doing nothing to solve them; they were merely being driven deeper inside me.

My black mood worsened when Yuki went away. She said nothing to me about it, just vanished one day. In the morning I heard her voice and her tread while we were at training. I heard her go to the front door and leave without bidding anyone farewell. I listened all day for her return, but she did not come back. I tried asking casually where she was; the replies were evasive and I did not want to question Akio or Gosaburo directly. I missed her deeply but was also relieved that I no longer had to face the question of whether to sleep with her or not. Every day since she had told me about Kaede I'd resolved I would not, and every night I did.

Two days later, while I was thinking about her during the meditation period at the end of the morning exercises, I heard one of the servants come to the door and call softly to Akio. He opened his eyes slowly and, with the air of calm composure that he always assumed after meditating (and which I was convinced was only assumed), he rose and went to the door.

"The master is here," the girl said. "He is waiting for you."

"Hey, Dog," Akio called to me. The others sat without moving a muscle, without looking up, as I stood. Akio jerked his head and I followed him to the main room of the house, where Kikuta Kotaro was drinking tea with Gosaburo.

We entered the room and bowed to the floor before him.

"Sit up," he said, and studied me for a few moments. Then he addressed Akio. "Have there been any problems?"

"Not really," Akio said, implying there had been quite a few.

"What about attitude? You have no complaints?"

Akio shook his head slowly.

"Yet, before you left Yamagata . . . ?"

I felt that Kotaro was letting me know he knew everything about me.

"It was dealt with," Akio replied briefly.

"He's been quite useful to me," Gosaburo put in.

"I'm glad to hear it," Kotaro said dryly.

His brother got to his feet and excused himself—the pressures of business, the need to be in the shop. When he had left the master said, "I spoke to Yuki last night."

"Where is she?"

"That doesn't matter. But she told me something that disturbs me a little. We did not know that Shigeru went to Mino expressly to find you. He let Muto Kenji believe the encounter happened by chance."

He paused but I said nothing. I remembered the day Yuki had found this out, while she was cutting my hair. She had thought it important information, important enough to pass on to the master. No doubt she had told him everything else about me.

"It makes me suspect Shigeru had a greater knowledge of the Tribe than we realized," Kotaro said. "Is that true?"

"It's true that he knew who I was," I replied. "He had been friends with the Muto master for many years. That's all I know of his relationship with the Tribe."

"He never spoke to you of anything more?"

"No." I was lying. In fact Shigeru had told me more, the night we had talked in Tsuwano—that he had made it his business to find out about the Tribe and that he probably knew more about them than any other outsider. I had never shared this information with Kenji and I saw no reason to pass it on to Kotaro. Shigeru was dead, I was now bound to the Tribe, but I was not going to betray his secrets.

I tried to make my voice and face guileless and said, "Yuki asked me the same thing. What does it matter now?"

"We thought we knew Shigeru, knew his life," Kotaro answered. "He keeps surprising us, even after his death. He kept things hidden even from Kenji—the affair with Maruyama Naomi, for example. What else was he hiding?"

I shrugged slightly. I thought of Shigeru, nicknamed the Farmer, with his openhearted smile, his seeming frankness and simplicity. Everyone had misjudged him, especially the Tribe. He had been so much more than any of them had suspected.

"Is it possible that he kept records of what he knew about the Tribe?"

"He kept many records of all sorts of things," I said, sounding puzzled. "The seasons, his farming experiments, the land and crops, his retainers. Ichiro, his former teacher, helped him with them, but he often wrote himself."

I could see him, writing late into the night, the lamp flickering, the cold penetrating, his face alert and intelligent, quite different from its usual bland expression.

"The journeys he made—did you go with him?"

"No, apart from our flight from Mino."

"How often did he travel?"

"I'm not sure; while I was in Hagi he did not leave the city."

Kotaro grunted. Silence crept into the room. I could barely hear the others' breathing. From beyond came the noon sounds of shop and house, the click of the abacus, the voices of customers, peddlers crying in the street outside. The wind was rising, whistling under the eaves, shaking the screens. Already its breath held the hint of snow.

The master spoke finally. "It seems most likely that he did keep records, in which case they must be recovered. If they should fall into Arai's hands at this moment, it would be a disaster. You will have to go to Hagi. Find out if the records exist and bring them back here."

I could hardly believe it. I had thought I would never go

there again. Now I was to be sent back to the house I loved so much.

"It's a matter of the nightingale floor," Kotaro said. "I believe Shigeru had one built around his house and you mastered it."

It seemed I was back there: I felt the heavy night air of the sixth month, saw myself run as silently as a ghost, heard Shigeru's voice: *Can you do it again?*

I tried to keep my face under control, but I felt a flicker in the smile muscles.

"You must leave at once," Kotaro went on. "You have to get there and back before the snows begin. It's nearly the end of the year. By the middle of the first month both Hagi and Matsue will be closed by snow."

He had not sounded angry before, but now I realized he was—profoundly. Perhaps he had sensed my smile.

"Why did you never tell anyone this?" he demanded. "Why did you keep it from Kenji?"

I felt my own anger rise in response. "Lord Shigeru did so and I followed his lead. My first allegiance was to him. I would never have revealed something he wanted kept secret. I was one of the Otori then, after all."

"And still thinks he is," Akio put in. "It's a question of loyalties. It always will be with him." He added under his breath, "A dog only knows one master."

I turned my gaze on him, willing him to look at me so I could shut him up, put him to sleep, but after one swift, contemptuous glance, he stared at the floor again.

"Well, that will be proved one way or the other," Kotaro replied. "I think this mission will test your loyalties to the full. If this Ichiro knows of the existence and contents of the records, he'll have to be removed, of course."

I bowed without saying anything, wondering if my heart had been hardened to the extent where I could kill Ichiro, the old man who had been Shigeru's teacher and then mine: I'd thought I wanted to often enough when he was chastising me and forcing me to learn, but he was one of the Otori, one of Shigeru's household. I was bound to him by duty and loyalty as well as by my own grudging respect and, I realized now, affection.

At the same time I was exploring the master's anger, feeling its taste in my mouth. It had a quality to it that was like Akio's more or less permanent state of rage against me, as if they both hated and feared me. "The Kikuta were delighted to discover Isamu had left a son," Kenji's wife had said. If they were so delighted why were they so angry with me? But hadn't she also said, "We all were"? And then Yuki had told me of her mother's old feelings for Shintaro. Could his death really have delighted her?

She had seemed at that moment like a garrulous old woman, and I had taken her words at face value. But moments later she'd allowed me a glimpse of her skills. She'd been flattering me, stroking my vanity in the same way she'd stroked my temples with her phantom hands. The reaction of the Kikuta to my sudden appearance was darker and more complex than they would have me believe: Maybe they were delighted with my skills, but there was also something about me that alarmed them, and I still did not understand what it was.

The anger that should have cowed me into obedience instead made me more stubborn—indeed, struck fire on that stubbornness and gave me energy. I felt it coiled inside me as I wondered at the fate that was sending me back to Hagi.

"We are entering a dangerous time," the master said, studying me as if he could read my thoughts. "The Muto house in Yamagata was searched and ransacked. Someone suspected you had been there. However, Arai has returned to

Inuyama now, and Hagi is a long way from there. It's a risk for you to return, but the risk of records coming into anyone else's hands is far greater."

"What if they aren't in Lord Shigeru's house? They could be hidden anywhere."

"Presumably, Ichiro will know. Question him, and bring them back from wherever they are."

"Am I to leave immediately?"

"The sooner the better."

"As an actor?"

"No actors travel at this time of year," Akio said scornfully. "Besides, we will go alone."

I'd been offering a silent prayer that he would not be coming with me. The master said, "Akio will accompany you. His grandfather—your grandfather—has died, and you are returning to Hagi for the memorial service."

"I would prefer not to travel with Akio," I said.

Akio drew his breath in sharply. Kotaro said, "There are no preferences for you. Only obedience."

I felt the stubbornness spark, and looked directly at him. He was staring into my eyes as he had once before: He had put me to sleep immediately then. But this time I could meet his gaze without giving in to it. There was something behind his eyes that made him flinch slightly from me. I searched his look and a suspicion leaped into my mind.

This is the man who killed my father.

I felt a moment of terror at what I was doing, then my own gaze steadied and held. I bared my teeth, though I was far from smiling. I saw the master's look of astonishment and saw his vision cloud. Then Akio was on his feet, striking me in the face, almost knocking me to the ground.

"How dare you do that to the master? You have no respect, you scum."

Kotaro said, "Sit down, Akio."

My eyes snapped back to him, but he was not looking at me.

"I'm sorry, master," I said softly. "Forgive me."

We both knew my apology was hollow. He stood swiftly and covered the moment with anger.

"Ever since we located you we have been trying to protect you from yourself." He did not raise his voice but there was no mistaking his fury. "Not only for your own sake, of course. You know what your talents are and how useful they could be to us. But your upbringing, your mixed blood, your own character, all work against you. I thought training here would help, but we don't have time to continue it. Akio will go with you to Hagi and you will continue to obey him in all things. He is far more experienced than you; he knows where the safe houses are, whom to contact and who can be trusted."

He paused while I bowed in acceptance, and then went on, "You and I made a bargain at Inuyama. You chose to disobey my orders then and return to the castle. The results of Iida's death have not been good for us. We were far better off under him than under Arai. Apart from our own laws of obedience that any child learns before they turn seven, your life is already forfeit to me by your own promise."

I did not reply. I felt he was close to giving up on me, that his patience with me, the understanding of my nature that had calmed and soothed me, was running dry. As was my trust in him. The terrible suspicion lay in my mind; once it had arisen there was no eradicating it: My father had died at the hands of the Tribe, maybe even killed by Kotaro himself, because he had tried to leave them. Later I would realize that this explained many things about the Kikuta's dealings with me—their insistence on my obedience, their ambivalent attitude to my skills, their contempt of my loyalty to Shigeru—

but at that time it only increased my depression. Akio hated me, I had insulted and offended the Kikuta master, Yuki had left me, Kaede was probably dead . . . I did not want to go on with the list. I gazed with unseeing eyes at the floor while Kikuta and Akio discussed details of the journey.

We left the following morning. There were many travelers on the road, taking advantage of the last weeks before the snow fell, going home for the New Year Festival. We mingled with them, two brothers returning to our hometown for a funeral. It was no hardship to pretend to be overcome by grief. It seemed to have become my natural state. The only thing that lightened the blackness that enveloped me was the thought of seeing the house in Hagi and hearing for one last time its winter song.

My training partner, Hajime, traveled with us for the first day; he was on his way to join a wrestling stable for the winter to prepare for the spring tournaments. We stayed that night with the wrestlers and ate the evening meal with them. They consumed huge stews of vegetables and chicken, a meat they considered lucky because the chicken's hands never touch the ground, with noodles made of rice and buckwheat, more for each one than most families would eat in a week. Hajime, with his large bulk and calm face, resembled them already. He had been connected with this stable, which was run by the Kikuta, since he was a child, and the wrestlers treated him with teasing affection.

Before the meal we bathed with them in the vast steamy bathhouse, built across a scalding, sulfurous spring. Masseurs and trainers mingled among them, rubbing and scrubbing the massive limbs and torsos. It was like being among a race of giants. They all knew Akio, of course, and treated him with ironic deference, because he was the boss's family, mixed with kindly scorn, because he was not a wrestler. Nothing was said about me, and nobody paid me any attention. They were absorbed in their own world. I obviously had only the slightest connection to it and therefore was of no interest to them.

So I said nothing, but listened. I overheard plans for the spring tournament, the hopes and desires of the wrestlers, the jokes whispered by the masseurs, the propositions made, spurned, or accepted. And much later, when Akio had ordered me to bed and I was already lying on a mat in the communal hall, I heard him and Hajime in the room below. They had decided to sit up for a while and drink together before they parted the next day.

I tuned out the snores of the wrestlers and concentrated on the voices below. I could hear them clearly through the floor. It always amazed me that Akio seemed to forget how acute my hearing was. I supposed he did not want to acknowledge my gifts, and this made him underestimate me. At first I thought it was a weakness in him, almost the only one; later it occurred to me that there were some things he might have wanted me to hear.

The conversation was commonplace—the training Hajime would undergo, the friends they'd caught up with—until the wine began to loosen their tongues.

"You'll go to Yamagata, presumably?" Hajime asked.

"Probably not. The Muto master is still in the mountains, and the house is empty."

"I assumed Yuki had gone back to her family."

"No, she's gone to the Kikuta village, north of Matsue. She'll stay there until the child is born."

"The child?" Hajime sounded as dumbfounded as I was.

There was a long silence. I heard Akio drink and swallow.

When he spoke again his voice was much quieter. "She is carrying the Dog's child."

Hajime hissed through his teeth. "Sorry, Cousin, I don't want to upset you, but was that part of the plan?"

"Why should it not have been?"

"I always thought, you and she . . . that you would marry eventually."

"We have been promised to each other since we were children," Akio said. "We may still marry. The masters wanted her to sleep with him, to keep him quiet, to distract him, to get a child if possible."

If he felt pain he was not showing it. "I was to pretend suspicion and jealousy," he said flatly. "If the Dog knew he was being manipulated, he might never have gone with her. Well, I did not have to pretend it: I did not realize she would enjoy it so much. I could not believe how she was with him, seeking him out day and night like a bitch in heat—" His voice broke off. I heard him gulp down a cup of wine and heard the clink and gurgle of the flask as more was poured.

"Good must come of it, though," Hajime suggested, his voice regaining some of its cheerfulness. "The child will inherit a rare combination of talents."

"So the Kikuta master thinks. And this child will be with us from birth. It will be raised properly, with none of the Dog's deficiencies."

"It's astonishing news," Hajime said. "No wonder you've been preoccupied."

"Most of the time I'm thinking about how I'll kill him," Akio confessed, drinking deeply again.

"You've been ordered to?" Hajime said bleakly.

"It all depends on what happens at Hagi. You might say he's on his last chance."

"Does he know that? That he's being tested?"

"If he doesn't, he'll soon find out," Akio said. After another long pause he said, "If the Kikuta had known of his existence, they would have claimed him as a child and brought him up. But he was ruined first by his upbringing and then by his association with the Otori."

"His father died before he was born. Do you know who killed him?"

"They drew lots," Akio whispered. "No one knows who actually did it, but it was decided by the whole family. The master told me this in Inuyama."

"Sad," Hajime murmured. "So much talent wasted."

"It comes from mixing the blood," Akio said. "It's true that it sometimes throws up rare talents, but they seem to come with stupidity. And the only cure for stupidity is death."

Shortly afterward they came to bed. I lay still, feigning sleep, until daybreak, my mind gnawing uselessly at the news. I was sure that no matter what I did or failed to do in Hagi, Akio would seize on any excuse to kill me there.

As we bade farewell to Hajime the next morning, he would not look me in the eye. His voice held a false cheerfulness, and he stared after us, his expression glum. I imagine he thought he would never see me again.

We traveled for three days, barely speaking to each other, until we came to the barrier that marked the beginning of the Otori lands. It presented no problem to us, Akio having been supplied with the necessary tablets of identification. He made all the decisions on our journey: where we should eat, where we should stop for the night, which road we should take. I followed passively. I knew he would not kill me before we got to Hagi; he needed me to get into Shigeru's house, across the nightingale floor. After a while I began to feel a sort of regret that we weren't good friends, traveling together. It seemed a waste of a journey. I longed for a companion, someone like Makoto or my old friend from Hagi, Fumio, with whom I could talk on the road and share the confusion of my thoughts.

Once we were in Otori land I expected the countryside to look as prosperous as it had when I had first traveled through it with Shigeru, but everywhere bore signs of the ravages of the storms and the famine that followed them. Many villages seemed to be deserted, damaged houses stood unrepaired, starving people begged at the side of the road. I overheard snatches of conversation: how the Otori lords were now demanding sixty percent of the rice harvest, instead of the forty percent they had taken previously, to pay for the army they were raising to fight Arai, and how men might as well kill themselves and their children rather than starve slowly to death when winter came.

Earlier in the year we might have made the journey more swiftly by boat, but the winter gales were already lashing the coast, driving foaming gray waves onto the black shore. The fishermen's boats were moored in such shelter as they could find, or pulled high onto the shingle, lived in by families until spring. Throughout winter the fishing families burned fires to get salt from the seawater. Once or twice we stopped to warm ourselves and eat with them, Akio paying them a few small coins. The food was meager: salt fish, soup made from kelp, sea urchins, and small shellfish.

One man begged us to buy his daughter, take her with us to Hagi, and use her ourselves or sell her to a brothel. She could not have been more than thirteen years old, barely into womanhood. She was not pretty, but I can still recall her face, her eyes both frightened and pleading, her tears, the look of relief when Akio politely declined, the despair in her father's attitude as he turned away.

That night Akio grumbled about the cold, regretting his decision. "She'd have kept me warm," he said more than once.

I thought of her sleeping next to her mother, faced with the choice between starvation and what would have been no more than slavery. I thought about Furoda's family, turned out of their shabby, comfortable house, and I thought of the man I'd killed in his secret field, and the village that would die because of me.

These things did not bother anyone else—it was the way the world was—but they haunted me. And of course, as I did every night, I took out the thoughts that had lain within me all day and examined them.

Yuki was carrying my child. It was to be raised by the Tribe. I would probably never even set eyes on it.

The Kikuta had killed my father because he had broken the rules of the Tribe, and they would not hesitate to kill me.

I made no decisions and came to no conclusions. I simply lay awake for long hours of the night, holding the thoughts as I would hold black pebbles in my hand, and looking at them.

The mountains fell directly to the sea around Hagi, and we had to turn inland and climb steeply before we crossed the last pass and began the descent toward the town.

My heart was full of emotion, though I said nothing and gave nothing away. The town lay as it always had, in the cradle of the bay, encircled by its twin rivers and the sea. It was late afternoon on the day of the winter solstice, and a pale sun was struggling through gray clouds. The trees were bare, fallen leaves thick underfoot. Smoke from the burning of the last rice stalks spread a blue haze that hung above the rivers, level with the stone bridge.

Preparations were already being made for the New Year

Festival: Sacred ropes of straw hung everywhere and dark-leaved pine trees had been placed by doorways; the shrines were filling with visitors. The river was swollen with the tide that was just past the turn and ebbing. It sang its wild song to me, and beneath its churning waters I seemed to hear the voice of the stonemason, walled up inside his creation, carrying on his endless conversation with the river. A heron rose from the shallows at our approach.

When we crossed the bridge I read again the inscription that Shigeru had read to me: *The Otori clan welcomes the just and the loyal. Let the unjust and the disloyal beware.*

Unjust and disloyal. I was both: disloyal to Shigeru, who had entrusted his lands to me, and unjust as the Tribe are, unjust and pitiless.

I walked through the streets, head down and eyes lowered, changing the set of my features in the way Kenji had taught me. I did not think anyone would recognize me. I had grown a little and had become both leaner and more muscular during the past months. My hair was cut short; my clothes were those of an artisan. My body language, my speech, my gait—everything about me was changed since the days when I'd walked through these streets as a young lord of the Otori clan.

We went to a brewery on the edge of town. I'd walked by it dozens of times in the past, knowing nothing of its real trade. *But,* I thought, *Shigeru would have known.* The idea pleased me: that he had kept track of the Tribe's activities, had known things that they were ignorant of, had known of my existence.

The place was busy with preparations for the winter's work. Huge amounts of wood were being gathered to heat the vats, and the air was thick with the smell of fermenting rice. We were met by a small, distracted man who resembled Kenji. He was from the Muto family; Yuzuru was his given name. He had not been expecting visitors so late in the year, and my presence and what we told him of our mission unnerved him. He took us hastily inside to another concealed room.

"These are terrible times," he said. "The Otori are certain to start preparing for war with Arai in the spring. It's only winter that protects us now."

"You've heard of Arai's campaign against the Tribe?"

"Everyone's talking about it," Yuzuru replied. "We've been told we should support the Otori against him as much as we can for that reason." He shot a look at me and said resentfully, "Things were much better under Iida. And surely it's a grave mistake to bring him here. If anyone should recognize him . . ."

"We'll be gone tomorrow," Akio replied. "He just has to retrieve something from his former home."

"From Lord Shigeru's? It's madness. He'll be caught."

"I don't think so. He's quite talented." I thought I heard mockery beneath the compliment and took it as one more indication that he meant to kill me.

Yuzuru stuck out his bottom lip. "Even monkeys fall from trees. What can be so important?"

"We think Otori might have kept extensive records on the Tribe's affairs."

"Shigeru? The Farmer? Impossible!"

Akio's eyes hardened. "Why do you think that?"

"Everyone knows . . . well, Shigeru was a good man. Everyone loved him. His death was a terrible tragedy. But he died because he was . . ." Yuzuru blinked furiously and looked apologetically at me. "He was too trusting. Innocent almost. He was never a conspirator. He knew nothing about the Tribe."

"We have reasons to think otherwise," Akio said. "We'll know who's right before tomorrow's dawn."

"You're going there tonight?"

"We must be back in Matsue before the snows come."

"Well, they'll be early this year, possibly before the year's end." Yuzuru sounded relieved to be talking about something as mundane as the weather. "All the signs are for a long, hard winter. And if spring's going to bring war, I wish it may never come."

It was already freezing within the small, dark room, the third such that I had been concealed in. Yuzuru himself brought us food, tea—already cooling by the time we tasted it—and wine. Akio drank the wine but I did not, feeling I needed my senses to remain acute. We sat without speaking as night fell.

The brewery quieted around us, though its smell did not diminish. I listened to the sounds of the town, each one so familiar to me, I felt I could pinpoint the exact street, the exact house, it came from. The familiarity relaxed me, and my depression began to lift a little. The bell sounded from Daishoin, the nearest temple, for the evening prayers. I could picture the weathered building, the deep green darkness of its grove, the stone lanterns that marked the graves of the Otori lords and their retainers. I fell into a sort of waking dream in which I was walking among them.

Then Shigeru came to me again as if from out of a white mist, dripping with water and blood, his eyes burning black, holding an unmistakable message for me. I snapped awake, shivering with cold.

Akio said, "Drink some wine, it'll steady your nerves."

I shook my head, stood, and went through the limbering exercises the Tribe use until I was warm. Then I sat in meditation, trying to retain the heat, focusing my mind on the night's work, drawing together all my powers, knowing now how to do at will what I had once done by instinct.

From Daishoin the bell sounded. Midnight.

I heard Yuzuru approaching, and the door slid open. He beckoned to us and led us through the house to the outer gates. Here he alerted the guards and we went over the wall. One dog barked briefly but was silenced with a cuff.

It was pitch-dark, the air icy, a raw wind blowing off the sea. On such a foul night no one was on the streets. We went silently to the riverbank and walked southeast toward the place where the rivers joined. The fish weir where I had often crossed to the other side lay exposed by the low tide. Just beyond it was Shigeru's house. On the near bank, boats were moored. We used to cross the river in them to his lands on the opposite side, the rice fields and farms, where he tried to teach me about agriculture and irrigation, crops, and coppices. And boats had brought the wood for the tearoom and the nightingale floor, listing low in the water with the sweet-smelling planks, freshly cut from the forests beyond the farms. Tonight it was too dark even to make out the mountain slopes where the trees had grown.

We crouched by the side of the narrow road and looked at the house. There were no lights visible, just the dim glow of a brazier from the guardroom at the gate. I could hear men and dogs breathing deeply in sleep. The thought crossed my mind: They would not have slept so had Shigeru been alive. I was angry on his behalf, not least with myself.

Akio whispered, "You know what you have to do?"

I nodded.

"Go, then."

We made no other plans. He simply sent me off as if I were a falcon or a hunting dog. I had a fair idea what his own plan was: When I returned with the records, he would take them—and I would be reported unfortunately killed by the guards, my body thrown into the river.

I crossed the street, went invisible, leaped over the wall,

and dropped into the garden. Immediately the muffled song of the house enveloped me: the sighing of the wind in the trees, the murmur of the stream, the splash of the waterfall, the surge of the river as the tide began to flow. Sorrow swept over me. What was I doing returning here in the night like a thief? Almost unconsciously I let my face change, let my Otori look return.

The nightingale floor extended around the whole house, but it held no threat to me. Even in the dark I could still cross it without making it sing. On the farther side I climbed the wall to the window of the upper room—the same route the Tribe assassin, Shintaro, had taken over a year ago. At the top I listened. The room seemed empty.

The shutters were closed against the freezing night air, but they were not bolted, and it was easy to slide them apart enough to creep through. Inside it was barely any warmer and even darker. The room smelled musty and sour, as if it had been closed for a long time, as if no one sat there anymore save ghosts.

I could hear the household breathing and recognized the sleep of each one. But I could not place the one I needed to find: Ichiro. I stepped down the narrow staircase, knowing its favorite creaks as I knew my own hands. Once below I realized the house was not completely dark as it had appeared from the street. In the farthest room, the one Ichiro favored, a lamp was burning. I went quietly toward it. The paper screen was closed, but the lamp threw the shadow of the old man onto it. I slid open the door.

He raised his head and looked at me without surprise. He smiled sorrowfully and made a slight movement with his hand. "What can I do for you? You know I would do anything to bring you peace, but I am old. I have used the pen more than the sword."

"Teacher," I whispered. "It's me. Takeo." I stepped into the room, slid the door closed behind me, and dropped to my knees before him.